Neve~~r~~

Ben, Frankie and the rest of the gang can't believe their eyes when they see the wire fence that shuts them out of Grace Park. They'd always played football there, and Ben's grandfather had too. But they're not going to let the Council build on *their* ground without a fight.

"Beautifully handled." *Guardian*

Also available in Lions

Gareth Owen

Never Walk Alone

LIONS

First published in Great Britain by
William Collins Sons & Co. Ltd 1989
First published in Lions 1991

Lions is an imprint of
the Children's Division, part of
HarperCollins Publishers Ltd,
77 Fulham Palace Road, London W6 8JB

ISBN 0–00–673343–3

Set in Plantin
Printed and bound in Great Britain by
William Collins Sons & Co. Ltd, Glasgow

For Denise – 1938-1987

I screamed, 'Frankie, over here.'

Frankie beat the Brazilian centre-half with an easy shrug of the shoulders and pumped the ball out to me on the wing. As I brought it under control and watched the full-back boring in, I knew this would be England's last chance to beat Brazil and win the World Cup.

Keep cool, I said to myself and feinted as if to cut inside; turned for the corner flag taking the full-back with me, whipped round again and made for goal. The full-back was stranded. Only the goalkeeper now. He was off his line, spreading himself. There was space past his left hand, not much but enough. Please let me hit it right. I drew back my right foot, but as I shot I heard my grandad calling.

'Ben, Ben, I have to get my pension.' He wheeled the pram across the grass towards where we were playing. The ball skidded off the side of my foot, missing the goal by a mile and ended up on the steps where the old Grace Park stand had once been.

Frankie came running up. 'How could you do that? How could you miss from there?' My little brother, Sam, was racing round the park doing forward rolls and shouting 'Brazil, Brazil,' like he'd seen them do on the telly.

I pointed at my grandad. 'It was Grandad. Just as I was going to score he shouted at me.'

'That means another replay,' Frankie said. 'That'll be the twenty-fifth. I don't think I can stand much more.'

Grandad came up to where we were standing. Baby Andrew had his thumb in his mouth and was dribbling down his chin. He was pink and his eyes were fast closed.

'Call that a shot?' said Grandad. 'You missed by a mile. I thought you were aiming for the thirty-three bus. I could have done better than that with a bucket over my head.'

'You called out to me just as I was about to shoot.'

'Excuses, excuses,' said Grandad. 'I had thousands shouting at me. I never missed like that.'

'No, Grandad,' I said.

Sam ran up with the ball in his arms.

'Hello, Grandad,' he shouted.

'Hello, Ben.'

'I'm Sam,' said Sam.

Grandad was always getting our names wrong.

'That's right,' said Grandad. He held his arms out wide and Sam lobbed the ball to him. Grandad trapped it and then flicked it up into his hands. He was over seventy but he could still control a ball.

'Now then, what have I told you?'

I knew he was going to tell me to keep my eye on the ball. That was the golden rule.

'Eye on the ball, Grandad,' said Sam.

'He's only right,' said Grandad looking round at Frankie, Carlton, Stokesy, Trev and me. 'He's only right. Eye on the ball. The golden rule, lads. The golden rule.' He looked round at what was left of Grace Park. The bits of terracing with grass and dock leaves sprouting through, the rusty sheets of corrugated iron that had once been the roof of the stand. At the far end where the kop had been there were now rows of allotments. I could see by the expression on his face that Grandad was back in the past. Any minute now he was going to tell us how he'd scored the penalty that had knocked Everton out of the Cup. Sam and me had heard it hundreds of times.

He shook his head and smiled.

'I never told you how I scored that penalty that put Everton out of the Cup, did I?'

'I've got to be going for me tea,' said Carlton. 'Me mum'll belt me, else.'

But Grandad didn't hear him.

'It were here. This very ground. Everton scored in the first five minutes. Lawton with his head. "Get in," he said. It went like a shell. I heard the net swish. I hated him. He were that good I hated him. He were brilliant, were Lawton. Head a ball faster than a mule could kick your backside. Then Scrapper crossed one. When Scrapper crossed like that you weren't supposed to miss. He could make the ball land on your head with the laces pointing away from you, so they wouldn't hurt when you headed it. I never liked to head a ball. Never did.

Only thing a head was good for in my opinion was putting your hat on. I just stuck my face in the road and the next thing I knew we were back in the game. We was level.'

Mr Halliday walked past with his dog.

'How do, Arthur?' said Mr Halliday.

'All right, Jim?' said Grandad.

Mr Halliday walked on and into the trees that led to Scarisbrick New Road and the Cottage Hospital. Grandad hardly hesitated.

'The game had replay written all over it. Then Scrapper put me through again. I could hardly lift me boots it were that muddy. It were like treacle in their penalty area. You could have buried three elephants in there and nobody would have noticed. I said to that ball, I said "Come here, you," I said. I stretched for it. Next thing, I was flat on my face in the mud and whistle was going. Coulter had brought me down. Penalty! Our Skipper said, "This one's yours, Arthur." I was looking the other way. I didn't want to know about it. In the end it was case of having to. I thought, if I miss this, nobody in town will talk to me for the rest of my life. I were that scared I thought of hitting it with my eyes shut.'

He looked round and then down at the ground.

'It would have been about here, the penalty spot.'

We all looked down as if we expected to see a blob of white on the grass. Then back up at Grandad. He dropped the ball on the ground and trapped it.

'I ran up. I was saying to myself, "Imagine it's a practice game, Arthur lad." There was fifty thousand there and they was all looking at me. They hadn't come to see me miss a penalty. I ran up. I can't remember hitting it. To this day, I can't remember. Next thing Ted Sagar was picking it out of the back of the net and we were on our way to Wembley.'

Grandad side-footed the ball. It flew through the two sticks we used for goals and knocked up against the pram. Baby Andrew woke up and started crying.

Grandad put his hand on my shoulder. 'Crikey, I nearly forgot. That's what I came for. Your mum wants you to take the baby back to our house. I have to get me pension. I'll be along directly.'

We walked over towards the pram. Baby Andrew's face was red and wrinkled. His fists were clenched tight and his mouth was wide open and full of bawling.

I hated wheeling a pram around. If anybody from school saw me they'd laugh and make stupid remarks. It wasn't Andrew's fault. He couldn't help being a baby.

'Oh Grandad, do I have to?'

'It won't take you long,' said Grandad. 'I might be back before you. She had an audition or summat. Margarine, she said. And your dad's had to go to Arkwright's to see if there's a job going.'

'Margarine?' I said. 'Is that a play?'

'Play? I don't know. I don't know what she's

on about half the time. I don't know. Don't seem right to me, her going out to work and your dad at home. I wouldn't have stood for it. Neither would Cissie. D'you remember your grandma?'

'Of course I do. You asked me that yesterday, Grandad.'

'Memory like a colander.' Grandad put his thumb under Baby Andrew's armpit. 'Google google google,' he said. Baby Andrew stopped crying for a moment and then started again, louder than ever.

'Mum only does it because Dad can't get a job,' I said.

'That's as maybe. Anyway, you look to him. How's the enemy?' He took his watch out of his waistcoat pocket. There were three thick gold medals hanging from the chain.

'Look at that time. I'll be off.' He held the watch to me.

'Did I ever show you me football medals?'

He'd showed them to me yesterday and twice the week before.

'Yes, Grandad.'

'Ah. What about the scrapbook with all the photographs? You've never seen that, have you?'

'You showed me that too, Grandad.'

'Did I really? I must be going doolally.' He put his watch away. 'I'd best be off or they'll be closed.'

Behind me I could hear Carlton and the rest of them arguing about whether there should be extra time or a replay. I watched Grandad walking slowly towards the road. His back was bent and his legs were bandy. Real footballer's legs. There was a man in a green mackintosh using a tripod to measure the park. Grandad said, 'How do?' He was always talking to people he'd never met before. The man looked up in surprise.

'Who's that fella Grandad's talking to?' asked Sam.

'Grandad talks to everybody,' I said.

It was true. You'd be sitting with him in a bus or a café and within five minutes he'd told complete strangers his whole life story. He could be bad tempered and embarrassing but I loved him. Just before he disappeared into the trees I called after him.

'Grandad.' He didn't hear but the man he was talking to nudged him.

Grandad turned and waved and smiled.

'I'll look at your medals tonight,' I shouted. 'And the photos.'

I don't think he heard me but he lifted his hand. He probably thought I was shouting goodbye.

'He's getting really deaf,' said Sam.

'That's why he speaks so loud.'

I could hear nearly everything he was saying even though he was nearly fifty yards away.

'I played here, you know. Yes. This is where the Town played in them days. That was when they was in the second division, before they got too big for their boots and moved to the new ground. I've

13

seen fifty thousand in here. Aye. Them's my two grandsons there. Two lads. Spend a lot of time with me. Their mam's an actress. Plays piano too. She's away a lot. Doing margarine this afternoon. How old d'you think I look . . . Do you? Well, I'm ten years older. Now then. Have you ever seen a medal like this?'

The man had given up measuring. He packed up his tripod and walked with Grandad towards the wood. I could still hear Grandad's voice going on with his story.

'. . . Anyway, the Skipper said, "You take it, Arthur." I was looking the other way. I didn't want to know. I didn't want to know. Thought of taking it with my eyes shut. I ran up and there it was in the back of the net and we were on our way to the Final . . .'

Grandad disappeared into the wood still talking. I had to watch him till he was gone. I always do that with people. I have this feeling that if I don't watch them till the very last moment, maybe I'll never see them again. The dark was starting to come down on the wood. I turned and walked back to where the rest were still arguing.

'We still haven't decided what we're going to do,' said Trev.

There was a long silence. Nobody knew.

'Ask Frankie,' I suggested.

Frankie was sitting on a broken turnstile pretending not to have heard.

'Ask Frankie, ask Frankie,' said Trev in a stupid voice. 'You want to ask Frankie everything.

You ought to get wed, you two.' I suppose, after Frankie, Trev was my best mate, but sometimes he made me sick. Really sick.

'Shut up, you,' I said, showing him a fist.

Trev just laughed.

I said, 'Why don't we have one last replay?'

'I don't want another replay,' said Frankie. 'You know it won't be the last. There'll be another one and another one. I want this to be the last. I want to do something else. I'm getting fed up with you lot.'

'This will be the last. We just play until it's over. First team to score three goals.'

'What happens if we both score three goals?' said Stokesy.

'Stupid.'

'You can't both score three goals.'

'You can,' said Stokesy, 'you can. Teams draw three-three, don't they, Trev? Don't teams draw three-three?'

'*First* team to score three goals, Cement Head. Both teams can't score three goals at the same time. It's impossible.'

Stokesy wrinkled his forehead. I could see he was thinking hard about it.

'What if it goes on all night?' said Carlton.

'We carry on.'

'Till it's over.'

'Till it's over.'

'What if it lasts a year?'

Frankie and me shouted. 'We carry on.'

'What if we all die of old age?'

We all shouted. 'We carry on.' Then everybody started laughing again.

'Next Friday,' said Frankie.

'I'm on holiday.'

'Friday after.'

'Friday after.'

'Three o'clock.'

'See you.'

'See you.'

Trev and Carlton walked off, their arms round each other. I could hear them saying over and over, 'We carry on,' and then laughing like mad. I could see it was going to be a new catch phrase.

'Bet I'll race you home,' said Sam, and started running.

'Give you a start,' said Frankie.

We crossed the road and made our way towards the school playing fields.

'Did you mean it that you didn't want to play any more?' I said.

'Of course. I don't say things unless I mean them,' said Frankie.

'You mean this game or ever?'

'After this game and then never.'

I thought about that. It wouldn't be the same game without Frankie.

'Why?'

'I want to do something different. Be somebody different.'

'Like what?'

'Oh, I don't know yet. I just get fed up with you lot sometimes.'

I wondered if Frankie got fed up with me.

'Fed up with all of us?'

'What you mean is, am I fed up with you?'

'No I didn't.'

Frankie laughed, head back looking at the sky. 'All that rolling about and stupidity.'

I quite liked all the rolling about and stupidity. Rolling about and stupidity was about what I was best at.

I nodded. 'Yeah, it's stupid,' I said.

'I suppose I'm fed up with doing the same things. It's like being in the same boat all the time. Eating the same food. Seeing the same faces. I want to get on another boat. Just to see what it's like. Anyway, I can't spend my whole life playing football. There's other things. Different things. Somewhere, out there.'

We crossed the school playground, walking towards the scaffolding where they were building the new drama studio. The door opened and Alan Maitland and his gang came out. They walked towards us laughing and putting on stupid voices. Just because they'd been in a few plays they thought they were something special. They thought they were great actors. But they weren't really. I'd seen them doing *A Christmas Carol* last year and they'd been hopeless. All putting on stupid voices so you couldn't understand what they were supposed to be saying. Afterwards, they all walked about as if they thought everybody was looking at them. But nobody was really. I hated acting. Alan Maitland had been all right, though.

17

He'd been this miserable old man called Scrooge who won't give anybody a day off at Christmas, even the dad of this little kid with one leg. Alan Maitland was the kid who'd picked me to play at Grace Park when I'd first started going over there. Then he'd left. Maybe he thought he was too good to play football. Perhaps he thought he was too old to be kicking around with a bunch of kids like us. He'd only been back to Grace Park once, about a year ago. He'd run on to the field and tried to score but the ball had skidded off his boot and missed by a mile. I'd shouted after him, 'Ah useless,' and he'd walked off as if he hadn't heard; as if he'd meant to kick it into the trees.

The one I really hated was Betty Mallard. She was always talking in this dead loud voice, making nasty comments about people. She thought she was really funny but she wasn't at all, really. She had this long neck that always looked a bit red. As though she'd just had her hair cut.

As we walked past, she said in this dead sarcastic voice, 'Somebody's come late to audition for the play. What a pity.' She didn't look at me and Frankie but there was no one else around.

'Just ignore her,' said Frankie. But I couldn't.

'You talking to me?' I said.

Betty Mallard looked round as if she was surprised. 'Did someone speak? I thought I heard a coarse voice.'

'I wouldn't want to be in your play,' I said.

She carried on looking round as if I wasn't there. 'There it is again. The same voice. Unless it was a pig grunting.'

'Who you calling a pig?' I said. 'I wouldn't want to be in your stupid play anyway.'

'How would you possibly know it's stupid? You're too stupid to know.'

'If you're in it, it must be stupid.'

Brian Ogden looked at me. He wore big flashy glasses and a long scarf.

'We are witty, aren't we? His second name must be Oscar Wilde.'

I didn't know who Oscar Wilde was. Alan Maitland and Betty Mallard started laughing, as though he'd said something really clever. They were always doing that. Laughing about things you didn't know anything about.

Frankie came up and stood beside me, throwing the ball from hand to hand.

'What about your girlfriend?' said Betty Mallard.

Frankie was looking at the ground.

'I'm not his girlfriend,' she said. Then looked Betty straight in the eye. 'But he's a friend.'

Alan Maitland was looking at Frankie. 'We could do with more girls in the play we're doing now. To do some dancing. I could ask Mr Backhouse if you like.'

'I don't think so,' said Frankie.

'Why?'

'If I wanted to be in the play I'd ask Mr Backhouse myself.'

'Don't think we'd want a tart who played football in the play, anyway,' said Betty Mallard.

She shouldn't have called Frankie a tart. Betty Mallard was always doing things like that.

Frankie didn't seem angry, at all. She looked straight at Betty Mallard.

'There's nothing wrong with football. Football can be quite useful, Betty. For example, it can help you to get out of the way when somebody throws the ball at you.' And she hurled the ball straight into Betty Mallard's face. Betty fell back, screaming. I think she would have gone for Frankie but Alan Maitland held her back. He looked at Frankie. 'You might think about an audition, though. Bring Curly along, too.' He threw the ball back gently to Frankie.

Frankie just looked at him, rubbing her hand over her short red hair. They walked off.

Mr Backhouse came out of the drama studio. He unlocked the door of his car and started the engine. He wound down the window and said to Frankie, 'Francesca, when are you going to give up this barbarian game and join the theatre club?'

'I don't know,' said Frankie.

'I know this is the emancipated twentieth century and you probably think I'm an old-fashioned fuddy duddy but I can't help thinking it's all wrong. Don't you agree?'

'No,' said Frankie looking Mr Backhouse straight in the eye, but she was smiling.

'What do you mean? No, I'm not an old-fashioned fuddy duddy, or no, you don't think it's wrong to play football?'

'I mean, no, I don't think it's wrong for me to play football.'

Mr Backhouse sighed. 'They still won't pick girls for the school team. Rules are rules, you know.'

'They ought to change the rules, then.'

Mr Backhouse laughed. 'What you ought to do is audition for the new play. No rules about keeping girls out of that.'

'Perhaps that's why I won't do it.'

'You mean, if I made a rule banning girls you'd be interested?'

Frankie laughed. 'Maybe,' she said.

Mr Backhouse knocked out his pipe. The ash fell on the playground.

'Well, think about it,' he said. 'Will you do that?'

'Yes,' said Frankie, 'I'll think about it.'

'Good,' said Mr Backhouse. He wound up his window and steered towards the school gates. The tyres whispered on the gravel.

We watched him go and walked across the playing fields. I whistled through my teeth and sneaked a look at Frankie. She was staring straight ahead.

'I wish I hadn't done that,' she said.

'What, said you'd do an audition?'

'No, thrown the ball at Betty Mallard.'

I'd liked her throwing the ball at her. As far

as I was concerned she could throw the ball at Betty Mallard all day.

'It was stupid. It was a stupid thing to do. I should have just walked away. Just turned and walked away. Tomorrow everybody will know.'

I thought, if I'd done that, I'd be really pleased if everybody knew. But I didn't say anything.

'It'll be one more mark against me. They'll say, "Did you hear what Frankie did to Betty Mallard? That's typical of her."' She pushed the football hard into my chest so that it made me gasp.

'And I don't want to be typical, Benbow.'

She stopped and looked at me. 'D'you understand?'

I didn't understand at all. 'Yes,' I said. ''Course I understand.'

A lot of the time I didn't understand what Frankie was on about. Maybe that's why she was my best friend.

I said, 'Are you really going to be in that play? With Alan Maitland and them?'

'I might be,' she said.

'What for?'

'It's another boat,' she said.

There was a silence. Then she said suddenly, 'Sam! He'll beat us.'

'He'll be there by now.'

'Not if we run,' said Frankie. 'Beat you to your house.'

And she was off and already five yards ahead before I'd caught on. I ran as fast as I could but she pulled away, her feet making hardly any noise at all.

I'd always had to run fast to keep up with Frankie, ever since she'd walked into our house that day four years ago.

2

When Frankie first came to our house I'd just been shot and was sliding down the bedroom wall trying to stop the blood from spouting out of the gunshot wound that Rico had just given me. Every night I died like that. Sometimes three or four times a night. I couldn't sleep properly until I'd been violently murdered. The mirror helped. It was a great mirror. If you wanted to watch yourself die there wasn't a better mirror anywhere. It had two wings so you could watch yourself die from the back, the side and the front, all at the same time. Wearing my dad's overcoat, the collar turned up, I'd saunter across the bedroom with my eyes half closed and sit down at the dressing table as if it was a card table in a night club in Chicago. I stared meanly into the mirror and snarled.

'OK, Rico, you cheated me one too many times.'

But Rico had a gun under the table. The force of the bullet knocked me off my feet, sending the chair flying. My mouth was open and I gasped for breath.

'You asked for it, Rico,' I whispered.

I let him have it without removing the gun

from my overcoat pocket. But I was dying. Back against the wall I staggered, my hands clutching the gaping wound in my chest. Moaning, I slid slowly down to the floor. My hands twitched for a second or two and then it was over. I was dead.

It was like that every night. Of course it wasn't always the same. There were endless variations. Sometimes I'd get shot in the back, killed running away from the bank robbery. Other times I'd reach the getaway car, pretending the mirror was the front windscreen. The shotgun blasted me through the rear window. My face would crash against the mirror and slide slowly down, eyes open but unseeing, my nose crushed sideways, mouth open and groaning. There were a hundred ways of dying violently and I was an expert at every one of them.

One night my mum had caught me. I'd got so carried away I hadn't noticed her standing in the bedroom doorway watching the whole performance. She was really upset. She thought I was going to grow up to be a criminal. Later, as I lay in bed, I could hear her telling my dad that it was all his fault.

'Look what's happening to that boy,' she shouted. 'Why can't he play normal games?'

'It is normal.'

'Normal for a boy. You don't see girls going round shooting themselves all day.'

'You're the actress,' my dad would say, 'that's where he gets it from.'

'Don't be ridiculous, when was I ever in a play where I shot somebody?'

'What about that Joan of Arc you did?'

'Don't talk nonsense. Joan of Arc didn't shoot herself.'

'No, but she set fire to herself.'

'She did not set fire to herself. If you'd listened to the play properly you'd have understood that. She was burnt to death. And you know who burned her? Men!'

'Don't blame me,' my dad protested, 'I wasn't there.'

'No, but if you had been you would have lit the first match.'

'What sort of example is that for a growing boy, to see his mother burnt to death every night?'

'If you remember, he didn't see me.'

'No, but he knew what was going on. He saw a rehearsal.'

'He was four, for God's sake.'

'Exactly,' said my father. 'Four years of age and he sees his mother going up in flames.'

Mum came back at him. 'It's all that rubbish on the telly you let him watch.'

'If you were home like a mother should be, maybe you'd be able to turn the rubbish off now and again.'

'How many nights wasn't I home? How many nights?'

'Thousands. When you should have been here looking after him you were too busy going up in flames on the stage.'

'That was one play. One play. You knew I'd never get the chance again. You agreed I should do it.' Mum was really upset now.

'Mother's place is in the home. That's where you should be.'

'Oh yes, and what are we supposed to live on? Air?'

'Don't bring that one up. It wasn't my fault I was made redundant.'

'Nobody's saying it's anybody's fault. Why does it have to be anybody's fault? It just makes sense for me to get work when I can if you're out of work.'

'Who had to make their tea tonight?'

'What's so terrible about that? Hundreds of husbands do it.'

'I'm not hundreds of husbands. I'm me.'

It went on for hours like that. It made Sam cry, but by the time I was nine I was used to it. To be honest I think that in a funny kind of way they enjoyed it. It was like listening to a bad tempered tennis match. Then I'd hear Mum crashing the notes on the piano with frustration. She was better at arguing but Dad was more persistent. Then the crash of notes turned into a tune. Mum would start singing and after a bit Dad would join in and then they'd be fine. Until the next time. Meanwhile, I was working on another sudden and violent death, only more quietly.

Then, this one night, as I was spitting words out of the corner of my mouth, I became aware of the reflection of a girl standing in the doorway. She had short red hair and very big staring eyes. The death scene stopped suddenly. I felt embarrassed. It was like being caught by Mum all over again. I pretended I hadn't seen her and started to make gargling sounds as if I had a bad throat that I was trying to cure. Then I looked round as if I was really surprised to see anybody and said, 'Oh, hello. I've got this dead bad throat.' I gargled and coughed a bit more to show how bad my throat was. She didn't say anything. Just stood there looking at me with her big staring eyes. I gargled a bit more. I don't think she was taken in. I was so busy coughing and being embarrassed that it hadn't occurred to me that there was something unusual about having a strange girl carrying a suitcase, staring at me through my bedroom door. I couldn't go on coughing and gargling for ever. There was a silence. She didn't say anything. Just stared. It seemed to go on for ever. Then she put the suitcase down.

'Didn't they tell you?' she asked.

I didn't know what she was talking about. 'Tell me what?'

'About me. Didn't they tell you I was coming to stay?'

I shook my head.

She shouted down the stairs. 'Mummy, the boy doesn't know.'

Nobody answered.

'They're in the garden,' she said.

Then I remembered. Mum had told me that

an old friend of hers was coming to stay. She hadn't said anything about a daughter, though.

I shook my head again. Then the red-headed girl started talking. When she started I thought she was never going to stop. She went on and on in a flat, breathless, matter of fact voice. And all the time her wide, unblinking eyes stared at me.

'I'm sorry you're going to have to leave your bedroom. Your mum said I should sleep here with my mum. Do you mind a lot? I don't mind sleeping downstairs on the couch but there wouldn't be room for Mum. I bet you're wondering why I'm here. My name's Francesca but everybody calls me Frankie. I'm coming to stay for a bit while my mother and father decide whether to get a divorce. He's gone away to think about it. It's called a trial separation. I heard them talking about it. He told me it was because of his work but I know that's not the real reason. I wish they'd tell the truth, don't you? Perhaps I'll never see him again or maybe just once a month like Sarah at school. My mum says she's going to study again. She wants to be an architect. When she's qualified she'll be able to put a big brass plate with her name and some letters on outside the front door. I think grown-ups are very silly sometimes, don't you? But I'm not going to cry about it, so you needn't look so worried. Your mum and mine were friendly a long time ago. I think they were at drama school together, so she thought I could stay here. I won't be a nuisance. Do your parents fight a lot? I'm never going to get married. What's your name? You don't want me here, do you? I can tell by your face.'

She stopped as suddenly as she'd begun and stared at me. Her eyes were violet. Then she looked at the wall and bit her lip. Tears started to come but she wasn't making any sound. She rubbed her eyes with her fists and said, 'You hate me, don't you?'

And that was the first time I ever saw Frankie.

She was right about one thing. I did hate her. I hated the way she looked. I hated the way she talked. And I hated the way she and her mum had taken over my room. I had to take all my pictures down and everything out of my drawers and go and sleep in Sam's room. It was only half the size of mine and it had to hold two of us. Most of all I missed my mirror. I couldn't get murdered in Sam's room. It would have given him nightmares. I kept wondering if Frankie had told anybody at school how she'd caught me that first time I'd seen her. I could just hear her stupid voice telling them. 'And d'you know what the idiot does? He actually talks to himself. Sits in front of the mirror talking to himself!' If I caught her at it I'd kill her.

Sam and me would have rows and fights because he didn't want me putting my stuff all round his room. He thought it was his room. I understood what he was going through. Lots of the time I'd go and stay with my grandad in Dacey Road just round the corner. That was before Grandma died. It was quiet there. Quiet and peaceful. There were no fights with Sam. No Mum and Dad arguing all the time and, best of all, there wasn't this stupid girl sitting opposite me at the table and taking over our house. I liked it at Grandad's.

At first, my mum said I had to walk Frankie to Junior School and look after her.

'She's new at the school. You can show her the ropes. She's looking after Sam, so you jolly well look after her.'

I dreaded that walk to school every morning. I'd have nightmares about it. Big Halsey and Andy Wall and the rest of his mates would be leaning over the school wall pulling faces, making loud kissing noises with the back of their hands and shouting stupid remarks like, 'Here comes the bridegroom'. Stuff like that. After school, I'd nip out early so I wouldn't meet her. I'd tell my mum I'd lost them on the way. All this time I never spoke to her unless I had to. She didn't seem to mind. Nothing seemed to bother her much. Even Big Halsey shouting his daft remarks. She'd just wheel into the playground holding Sam's hand. After a bit I started walking on the other side of the road. Later I started going the long way round to school, just so that I wouldn't be seen walking with her. She didn't seem to notice or if she did she didn't let it show. That made it even more annoying. Big Halsey and them still made fun of me. That was the trouble with them two. Once they got their teeth into you they never let go. They were like terriers. The only way to get them to stop was to fight them. It was a waste of time doing that, though, because Big Halsey was in the top class and twice as big as me. I might have been able to beat them if Trev had been with me. But he was a bigger coward than I was. In fact, he stopped being seen with me in case Big Halsey started picking on him too. That was the kind of mate he was.

One afternoon, as I was taking the long way home from school over the sandhills, I had the bad luck to run into Andy Wall. He started shouting out his usual remarks. 'Where's your girlfriend?' and 'Hello, lover boy'. All that usual kind of stuff. He'd forgotten Big Halsey wasn't with him. All the hatred and anger I'd been storing up for about three weeks boiled over. Andy Wall was standing on the top of his sandhill with his hands in his pockets, jeering. I ran up the hill towards him. At first he didn't understand what was happening and kept on shouting his stupid remarks at me. He'd been so used to getting away with it, with having Big Halsey with him, that he didn't think of running away. When he realized what was happening his face changed and he turned to run. By then it was too late and, anyway, the sand stopped him running fast. His arms were up in the air and he was having to pull his legs really high to get them out of the sand. He looked like someone trying to run through water. All the time, too, he kept looking round with his mouth wide open to see if I was still after him. He looked really comical. If I hadn't been so mad I would have probably laughed at him. I was having a job catching him, too. I hadn't been in a fight for about three years. The last time had been when Marion Archard had beaten me up just after I'd gone into the Juniors. She said it was because she liked me. The only fights I'd been in since then had been those in my own bedroom and usually I'd ended up being shot. This fight wasn't like the ones I'd seen on telly, either, where two blokes just stand up and hit each other on the chin. For a start, Andy Wall had his back to me and he was running away.

At the bottom of the hill he fell, rolled over, then stumbled to his feet again. I aimed a punch round his head, hoping to hit his jaw. But I missed and hit him on the back of the head instead. It didn't half hurt my hand. Andy Wall seemed really surprised. He held his hand over his head and shouted, 'That hurt, man. You hit me on the head.' Then I hit him again. I meant to hit him on the face but he ducked his head down and I caught him on the shoulder instead. He fell on the floor and I rolled on top of him. His knee caught me on the nose and I felt my eyes watering with the pain. When I'd had the fight in my bedroom it hadn't hurt like that. I asked him if he wanted to give in, hoping he'd say yes. It was stupid, really, because I'd hardly touched him and there was blood pouring out of my nose and all over the sand. Andy Wall didn't hear me, anyway. He was shouting, 'Halsey, Halsey, over here. Help, help.' Trying to make me believe that Big Halsey was around. But I knew that one.

33

He rolled over and my face hit the ground really hard. My mouth was full of sand and tasted of gritty blood. I lashed out wildly and my fist landed in something soft. I hoped it was Andy Wall. It was. I'd caught him in the stomach. He made a loud gasping noise as the air came out of him, and started moaning. I was wishing like mad he'd give in. I had my arm round his throat. I loosened it a bit so he could get up and run away. Then the fight would be over. I thought what I'd do would be to run after him for a bit, pretending I was trying really hard to catch him. Then I'd stop and shout that I'd get him next time. But he didn't even try to get away. He just lay on top of me, moaning. In the end I had to take my arm off his throat and push him off. I lay in the sand, gasping. He was half sitting up, his back to me covering the back of his head with his hands. He was moaning and crying to himself. I didn't want to hit him any more. We sat there, side by side, breathing heavily.

Then I saw something rolling down the hillside towards me. At first I thought it was a dog. The next minute all the breath was knocked out of my body and a big weight was lying on top of me. It was Big Halsey. As soon as he saw he wasn't alone and that he might be on the winning side, Andy Wall stopped moaning and began laying into me with both fists. There was a terrible pain in my ankle. I looked down. Big Halsey had his face in my leg and was biting my ankle as hard as he could. Big Halsey was a bit simple but he was bigger than the rest of us. He wore spectacles and had a lumpy sort of face like a potato. He always wore a suit. It was always the same worn, blue suit. I think it was because he was so big he could wear his dad's old suits. Now here he was trying to bite my leg off. My eyes were gritty with sand and I was swallowing blood. I lashed out as hard as I could with my foot. Big Halsey sprawled backwards, his spectacles knocked across his face. In a second he was back on top of me, pinning me down with the weight of his body. Andy Wall was thumping me whenever he could see my face. Blood was coming off my ear. I thought, my mum'll kill me if I get blood on this shirt. I must have been crying as well. I didn't want to but I couldn't help it.

Suddenly, someone else was there banging away at Big Halsey's back and screaming. It was Frankie. Sam was standing halfway down the sandhill with his hands behind his back, just watching. Big Halsey started thumping Frankie instead of me. Big Halsey would thump anything. He didn't care if it was a boy or a girl or a dog. I don't think he knew the difference. If it had been in one of those kids' books Frankie and me would have beaten them and we'd have been good friends for ever and walked round the school playground like conquering heroes. But it wasn't like that. After a bit, Andy Wall ran off because Frankie scratched all the left side of his face and Big Halsey wandered off because he got bored. Even as he walked along, Frankie was hanging on to him with one hand and trying to thump him with the other. But she couldn't reach his face. In the end he swung her off and she rolled under a hedge.

The fight was over.

Nobody had won and nobody had lost. Halsey would think he'd won and perhaps he was right. I hoped that maybe they'd been hurt enough not to risk another fight. Andy Wall would think twice about it. As the two of them dawdled away towards the railway bridge we shouted insults until they were out of sight.

I was a mess. There was blood over my face and shirt and my clothes and eyes were full of sand. Frankie was still lying down in the hedge where Big Halsey had thrown her. Her blouse was torn and the right side of her face was swollen. She was looking at the ground, panting. She wasn't crying, though. I wondered if she expected me to help her up or to start being friends with her. Perhaps she expected me to thank her for helping me out in the fight. But I wasn't going to do that. You didn't do that to girls. If she wanted to be friends with me she was going to have to ask me first. Then I'd think about it.

I shouted at her, 'I didn't need you, you know. I could have beaten them on me own if you hadn't joined in.'

She didn't say anything. She stood up slowly and brushed the dirt off her jeans.

I felt a pain shoot through my ankle and rolled my sock down. Where Big Halsey had bit me was a row of teeth marks and blood was coming through. Frankie looked at it.

'Where he bit me,' I said. I wasn't going to tell her it hurt.

She took out her hankie and went to wrap it round my ankle. I pulled away. 'I don't want that,' I said.

'You might get rabies,' she said.

I had this sudden picture of Big Halsey wearing his big suit but with a dog's head. I nearly laughed but just stopped myself in time. Frankie put the hankie in her pocket. She didn't seem bothered.

Sam was standing by the railway line, swaying slowly from side to side and watching us. I went to take his hand but he pulled away and put both hands to his face.

'Be like that,' I said.

I walked off home. I wanted to look back to see if they were following but I forced myself not to.

Later, Frankie came home. Sam was holding her hand. I could hear her in the kitchen washing the blood off her face. She told my mum how her blouse had got torn doing P.E. at school. At tea-time I didn't even look at her. If she was expecting me to be sorry she was going to have to wait a long time.

After, we never mentioned the fight. It was something we just never talked about. But it had made a difference. There was something between us now. Something that was secret and that we shared. We used to talk a bit; not straight away but after a week or two. It wasn't the sort of conversation I'd have with Trev or Carlton, it was too polite for that. But it was better than ignoring one another. Then, three weeks later, we walked up to the school gates together, Frankie and me. Big Halsey was there as usual with Andy Wall. They looked but they didn't say anything. We walked through the school gates side by side. I didn't say anything but I knew that something was different.

But what really changed things was Big Halsey and the werewolf.

After that the whole world was different.

3

It happened like this. Mum had gone out with Frankie's mum to look at a smaller house in town she was thinking of buying. Dad was giving Baby Andrew a bath, Sam was in his room reading a comic and Frankie and me were watching a film about a werewolf on the television. It was the first part of a two-part series. I thought it was pretty stupid but Frankie loved horror films. She lay on her front on the carpet with her face in her hands, her eyes wide open, watching every move. She was really pleased because the sequel to the film was being shown the next night. 'Two horror films in one week!' she said. 'What bliss.' She could hardly contain herself.

In this film, *The Curse of the Werewolf*, a man with glasses who worked in a chemist shop in Bavaria kept changing into a wolf. You'd know it was about to happen because this wild look would come into his eyes and hair would start growing all over his chest and face. Then his hands would change into big paws with great hooked claws on the end. Once he was a wolf, he'd go out and kill people all over the place. It was to do with the moon, really. As soon as this man saw the moon sailing across the sky, he'd start becoming a wolf. It wasn't scary at all, really. Even Frankie got bored and started laughing whenever this wolf hair started sprouting out of the man's shirt. Every time the moon came out it was obvious what was going to happen. The man would look up at the moon, tear his shirt open and start howling. After a bit we both started doing it as well. We cupped our hands to our mouths and gave a long mournful howl. 'Aaaaaaaaaaaaaooooooooh.' In the end we were doing it whenever he appeared. Like, he went into a shop to buy an ice cream and we'd both go 'Aaaaaaaaaaaaaooooooooh'. In the end Sam heard us and he started doing it as well. 'Aaaaaaaaaaaaaooooooooh' all over the place. All three of us. We were in hysterics. As usual, though, Sam got stupid and started doing it really loud all the time so it stopped being funny. Dad got fed up with the noise in the end and made Sam go to bed. Then we started again, only quietly so no one would hear. I found I could do it really well. Especially if I cupped my hands round my mouth. Frankie couldn't do it as well. It was too high pitched. Also she kept breaking down and laughing all the time. It didn't seem to bother her at all that I was better at it than she was. If it had been the other way round it would have really annoyed me. But she didn't mind at all. She said I sounded more like a wolf than the real one. So I made the noise more and more. It was true, I did sound like a wolf.

Then, right at the end of the film, the man appeared on some sandhills wearing an awful suit. The sandhills reminded us straight away of the fight we'd had. But neither of us said anything. There was something about the man. I couldn't think what it was. He took off his specs and cleaned them on his hankie.

Then Frankie said, 'He looks just like Big Halsey.'

She was right.

'Or his brother,' I said.

'He's got Big Halsey's suit on.'

We both started laughing. Then Frankie went quiet. This look came over her face and her eyes started to shine. Later I got to recognize that look. It meant that she had an idea, that something was about to happen. But at that time I didn't know her well enough. This was the first time it had happened.

She leaned forward and said in a whisper, 'Why don't we do it to Big Halsey?'

I didn't understand what she was on about.

'Do what?' I asked.

She explained the plan. It was a great plan. I couldn't believe that somebody I knew could think up anything so fantastic. I just looked at her in amazement.

The next day at school we started a rumour that a wolf had been heard roaming round the back gardens near Big Halsey's house. We said it had been in the papers, that Mrs Jackson at the paper shop had heard it, that Miss Abrahams, our teacher, had heard it too. It was amazing how the rumour went round. In fact during break in the afternoon Big Halsey came over to where me and Frankie were standing and asked us if we'd heard the rumour about the wolf.

Frankie was brilliant. She said she hadn't heard it herself but she said Miss Abrahams had told her class she'd heard a wolf. She said it absolutely straight-faced. I almost believed her myself. I could tell by Big Halsey's face that he was starting to believe it, too. He wrinkled his nose and said it was rubbish but I could tell he was starting to worry. Then Frankie said something that amazed me.

She said, 'Miss Abrahams doesn't tell lies. There she is on playground duty. Go and ask her if you like.'

She knew he never would.

Frankie looked at him, her eyes challenging him.

'I'll ask her if you like,' she said.

She walked over to where Miss Abrahams was standing and started talking to her. I don't know what she was saying but I could tell from watching Big Halsey that he thought it was all about the werewolf. As she walked back towards us she said in a loud voice,

'There you are, it's true, isn't it, Miss Abrahams? Only Graham Halsey doesn't believe it, Miss.'

Miss Abrahams nodded her head. 'Oh, it's true all right,' she said.

Frankie came over to where we were both standing.

'There you are,' she said.

Big Halsey tried to sneer but his face couldn't manage it.

Then Frankie said lightly, 'Anyway, I don't think it's a wolf. I think it's a werewolf. Like in that film last night.'

'Werewolf?' said Big Halsey. You could see he didn't know what a werewolf was. 'Oh yeah, one of them,' he said lightly, but I could tell he was worried.

'There's a sequel on tonight,' said Frankie. 'That means the story carries on.'

I thought she might make out that Big Halsey would be too scared to watch it. But she was cleverer than that.

She said, 'I'm not going to watch it. I'd be too scared.'

'Me, too,' I said.

Andy Wall came up and started talking to Big Halsey. Miss Abrahams blew the whistle. As we wandered off to line I heard Big Halsey saying, 'You heard about this werewolf? Miss Abrahams saw it last night.'

Frankie said, 'It's probably nothing. Anyway, they only come out in the moonlight.'

Andy Wall and Big Halsey walked away. I could see Big Halsey talking about it very seriously.

I said to Frankie, 'Did you really ask Miss Abrahams about the werewolf?'

''Course not,' she replied.

'Why did she say it was true, then?'

'I asked her if it was true that Mr Hocknell's wife had had a baby. I said Big Halsey didn't believe me.'

We walked into the school in our separate lines. Big Halsey was very quiet, for him.

That night we watched the sequel to the werewolf film. I practised my wolf calls.

When it was over we crept down to the bottom of our garden and made our way down Sandbrook Lane. It runs along the back of all these houses. The moon sailed big and white in and out of the clouds. Upstairs the back of Big Halsey's house was dark. There was a small gate next to a wooden shed. We opened it quietly and walked on tiptoe to the house. The curtains downstairs were drawn but we could hear the television. The kitchen door opened and Big Halsey's mother came out and called the cat in. We scuttled off into some bushes. She closed the door and locked it.

About five minutes later a light went on upstairs. We saw a shadow framed in the window. It stared out into the back garden. It was Big Halsey. A few seconds later there was another figure beside him. It was Big Halsey's mother. Then the curtains were drawn. We both watched, holding our breaths.

'Let him get into bed first.'

'I bet he goes to bed in his suit.'

We both started giggling.

After five minutes the light went out and Frankie nudged me.

'Now,' she whispered.

I cupped my hands round my mouth. The howl drifted out and hung on the air. I have to admit myself it sounded good. It echoed off the back of the house and hovered in the trees. Frankie had her face in her hands trying to keep in the laughter. I paused. Nothing moved. Everywhere was silent except for the sound of a faint breeze. Frankie nudged me again and I howled a second time; longer and more mournful this time. Suddenly the light went on and Big Halsey was at the window. He was wearing striped pyjamas. I could hear Frankie spluttering in the darkness beside me. I stopped. Big Halsey's mum was at his side again. They were both peering into the garden. I could hear them talking but couldn't make out what he was saying. But she seemed to be telling him off. After a minute she disappeared but the lights stayed on. Frankie took up a handful of earth and pebbles and crept out so that she was standing directly beneath the window. She whispered for me to howl again. This was a long, wailing, broken cry.

The window curtains parted again just as the howl died away. Big Halsey was there on his own. I let go another howl, louder than the last, and at the same time Frankie hurled the earth and pebbles upwards. They spattered on the bedroom window. We both heard Big Halsey give a long, faltering scream and then the curtains were pulled. We raced towards the garden gate and crouched in the shadow of the shed, doubled over with laughter. The kitchen door opened. Big

Halsey and his mum were framed in the light. We heard Big Halsey's mum shouting, 'Wolf, what wolf? You can see there's no wolf. Don't be bloody stupid,' and there was the sound of a loud slap and a cry from Big Halsey.

We ran down the lane towards our house, hardly able to run for laughing. Then a dark shape reared out of the darkness at us, barking and howling. We both screamed but it was only Mr Halliday's Alsatian. He was more frightened than we were. It made us laugh more than ever.

We were hanging on to each other. The moon sailed behind the clouds but the stars were bright. We both looked up through the darkness.

'Some of those stars are already dead,' Frankie whispered.

'Dead?'

'It's just their light you can see.'

I stared up into the night.

'They're so far away. Millions of millions of miles. By the time their starlight has reached us they're all dead.'

We stood looking upwards for a long time. A soft wind blew up from the shore. I could smell the pines. We stayed like that for a long time then walked up through our back garden and into the house.

4

After Big Halsey and the werewolf, Frankie and me always seemed to be together. I was still mates with Trev and Carlton but Frankie was the one I really got on with. At first some of the others used to shout remarks at us but when we didn't react they got bored and found somebody else to make fun of. Big Halsey didn't bother us any more because Frankie threatened to tell everybody what had really happened. Big Halsey couldn't stand kids laughing at him.

When Frankie was around there was always something happening, always a new craze. She never seemed to run out of things to do and she managed to make every new idea seem important even though you knew it might only last a week or sometimes even a day. I wondered if she ever found me dull to be with. I never mentioned it in case it put the idea into her mind, but I often wondered why she bothered with me. Maybe it was just because I was there; anyone else would have done just as well, but I happened to be the one that was around; I was convenient. Someone to follow where she led. And a lot of the time it was hard work keeping up with her. I was trying to think of a way of describing what it felt like to be with Frankie in those days and it came to me one day when I was coming in forty-third out of fifty-three in the Cross Country Race. It felt just like that. Breathless. Not breathless in your body but in your mind. It was a race and you had all your work cut out keeping her in sight.

One day she got a book out of the library all about China. She read it right through in one night. She was a really fast reader. About twice as fast as me. Sometimes we'd be reading a book together and I'd be still on the first paragraph and she'd be tapping her fingers with frustration and peeping at the next page. Anyway, after she read this book she was dead keen on anything that was to do with China. And of course I had to be the same. When we were seventeen we were going to go to China together. She went to Mayott's, the travel agents in town, and got a brochure about how to get there and how much it would cost. The girl behind the counter thought she was on to a really good thing. When she asked Frankie how long we'd be going for Frankie said, 'For ever.' The girl didn't know what to think. She was so surprised she said, 'That's a long time.' I could see Frankie repeating the phrase to herself, 'For ever is a long, long time.' She seemed to like it. The girl looked even more confused when she asked us when we were hoping to travel and Frankie said, 'Oh, in about seven years' time.'

After that, she made herself a Chinese calendar but instead of it going on for a year it was for seven years. It took up three walls of my old bedroom. Every day would be crossed off and on it she would write, 'Only six years, nine months, two weeks and three days until China Day.' She kept that calendar going for two years. She even started wearing one of her mum's long dressing gowns, pretending she was a Chinese lady. We even had to sit on the floor and drink tea like they did in China and every time we came in the house we had to take our shoes off. I didn't like tea much but I didn't want to be left out. All over her walls were pictures of China and she'd keep reciting names of Chinese towns and villages. She had an amazing memory. She would see how long she could go on reciting these names without repeating herself. You could ask her anything about China and she'd know the answer straight away. If she had a new idea, it didn't matter what time it was, she'd come and tell me about it. Sometimes she'd come into my room about three o'clock in the morning, shake me awake and say, 'Listen, Benbow, did you know the Chinese invented the compass?'

Well, I was only half awake so I couldn't understand what she was talking about.

'Compass,' she'd say. 'You know so you can find your way round the world in a boat.'

'Oh yeah,' I said.

'People over here think they're civilized. China was civilized while we were still running around in bear skins. But you try telling that to the people round here. They don't want to know. People are so locked up in their own cultural environment.

It makes you despair sometimes.' She used big words like that sometimes.

She even wanted to look Chinese. She spent hours in front of the mirror trying to make her eyes slant. She put her fingers in the corner and pulled them up. She thought if she did it long enough they'd stay there. Then she'd come padding into my bedroom, shake me awake and say, 'It worked for St Peter's foot. Why not with my eyes?'

She always went straight into a conversation like that. She never asked if you were awake or anything, just went straight in before you knew where you were.

'Peter's foot?' I said, through a blur of sleep.

'There's this statue of St Peter in Rome and all these pilgrims who go there kiss his foot as an act of penance. It's been kissed so many times that it's worn away. The stone's worn away. If it'll wear stone it's bound to work for skin. Look.' And she'd push her face down so I could see her eyes.

It was three o'clock in the morning and pitch dark. I was trying to work out why the Chinese were using a compass to get to Rome to kiss somebody's stone foot.

'Stupid Benbow. What I'm saying is, if you can wear away stone with your lips you're bound to be able to move your eyes because skin is softer than stone.'

I knew that was true. 'Skin's softer than stone all right,' I said. 'That's definitely true, Frankie.'

I tried to look intelligent, which was a bit of a waste of time since she couldn't see my face.

Frankie switched on my bedroom light. Sam turned over in his bed and groaned.

'D'you think they're moving, Benbow?'

'Moving?' I sat up and looked round the room nervously wondering what I was supposed to be looking for that might be moving.

'My eyes, d'you think they're moving?'

I peered forward, blinking. I couldn't see any difference but I'd say 'Yes' just to keep her happy. She'd look really pleased and give this big smile.

'I love you, Benbow,' she'd say and pat me on the top of the head as though I was a puppy. And then she was gone leaving me blinking and wide awake, trying to work out what was going on.

With the birthday money her mum sent her she bought an enormous map of China. We'd spend hours on the living room floor with it spread out, planning journeys. I'd follow her finger.

'I love maps, Benbow, don't you?'

I did, too. I liked reading all the names of the towns and the mountains and rivers. We'd spend hours going on imaginary journeys to all these different countries. Every week we'd go somewhere different. Frankie would spread out the map and say, 'Where to tonight then, Benbow?' And I'd choose.

'Yeah, I like maps,' I said.

'What do you like best about them?'

'Well . . .' I started to say, but I never got a chance.

'What I like about them is that you can travel hundreds of miles in a second. Thousands, thousands of miles just like that.' She whisked her hand across the map.

'Millions of miles,' I said, walking my fingers so that they ended up on the carpet.

'Now you're being stupid.'

She rolled over on her back and looked at the ceiling. Her eyes were almost closed. Whenever she did this I knew something big was coming. I tried hard to concentrate because I knew it would be a test of my intelligence.

'Just think, Benbow, in every one of those towns, in every one of those villages, there are people. People like you and me. And do you know, we'll never meet.'

I thought about that. It was a big thought. Frankie was always having big thoughts.

'And, and and . . .' she started. She was getting into gear. 'And maybe there's someone in China.'

'China,' I said trying to be helpful.

'In China now. No, not some*one*, some*two*. Why can't you say some*two*? If you can say some*one*, why not some*two*? Anyway, what I'm seeing is two people.'

I shifted my imagination so that I could see two people. There they were.

'A boy and a girl.'

'Like you and me.'

'Very good, Benbow. Like you and me. And what they're doing. What they're doing is . . .' She rolled over on her front and stared at me with her big violet eyes.

'What they're doing is . . .' I started confidently but I wasn't sure what they were doing. I didn't know what boys and girls in China did.

'They're looking at a map, too. It's a map of England. And they've picked out this town and do you know what they're saying? They're saying . . . they're saying, "I wonder if there's somebody there who's thinking about us." '

She stopped talking for a moment and there was a big silence that seemed to fill the world. I held my breath. The thought was too big for me. I tried hard to keep it boxed in but it kept escaping. I felt sick. Sick and excited all at once.

Then she'd leap up and be off into the garden with me trailing after her not wanting to miss anything. She'd be sitting in the car in the garage and we'd pretend to drive off to an unknown but distant destination.

But no matter how big China was it couldn't last for ever. Soon it was abandoned with all the other crazes and she'd be off on something new. Growing oaks from acorns, keeping spiders, painting part of the lawn blue, being a spy, flying, long distance swimming or mountain climbing. Mountain climbing. That was a big craze for a time. She'd think the greatest thing in the world would be to climb Everest. But it wasn't enough for Frankie just to climb a mountain. That would have been too easy.

'Too many people have already climbed it.' She stopped and thought for a second. 'Though, of course, I'd be the first girl to do it. I suppose that would be something.'

'I wouldn't, though. Be the first man, I mean.'

'No. What would make it good would be to be the first girl and to die in the attempt.'

I wasn't too keen on the bit about dying but I'd learned to keep my mouth shut. Frankie went on.

'And then, years later, another expedition would find our bodies, perfectly preserved by the ice and do you know what, Benbow? We'd be smiling.'

She gripped me by the shoulders.

'And do you know why we'd be smiling?'

I had no idea why two people dead on a mountain would be smiling but I was sure Frankie would have an answer. And she did.

'Because we'd be at the top, Benbow. At the top. We'd have conquered, conquered with our last breath; struggled to the very peak, knowing we were never going to descend alive. I'd pulled you up the last few inches and we'd looked at one another and because we knew we were the first boy and girl team to conquer that awesome peak we'd smiled and then,' and she paused and then whispered with awful intensity, 'died.'

There was another big silence and I'd feel

the familiar mixture of sickness and excitement building up in me.

'Would they leave us there or would they bring us down and give us a Christian burial?' I wasn't quite sure what a Christian burial was. I'd read the phrase somewhere and thought it might impress Frankie.

'Christian burial,' Frankie spat out with withering contempt. 'What, in a little churchyard with all our aunties and uncles? Never!'

'Never!' I shouted carried away by her contempt.

'No, they'd leave us there like carved statues as a warning and an inspiration to those who came after. And underneath would be a message carved out by a famous artist in letters of ice. And the letters would read, "They died but they conquered."'

'They died but they conquered,' I repeated, in a whisper.

But Frankie wasn't finished yet. She leaned towards me, her eyes wide.

'And that statue,' she whispered, 'would be there for ever.'

'For ever,' I repeated.

And then we both said with hushed voices, 'And for ever is a long, long time.'

Then we sat for a long time while the cars passed in the road, mothers did their shopping and the world kept on turning, thinking about this big thing called for ever. It was the biggest thought we'd ever had. I couldn't believe that everybody else hadn't been thinking about it as well. It was like when you've been ill in bed and go outside for the first time. Everything seems fresh and new and you almost have to learn to walk again. Well, that's what I felt like then and I knew Frankie was feeling the same. It became a catchphrase for us, especially if something bad happened. We'd say, 'For ever is a long, long time.' It seemed to put everything in perspective.

After ten months at our house Frankie went off to Belgium with her mum to stay with her dad. Frankie said it was a reconciliation. She was away for a year. It seemed funny without her. I started going round with Trev and Carlton again. But it wasn't the same. They never had any ideas. We'd spend whole days trying to think of something to do. One day Trev said, 'This holiday's going to go on for ever.'

Without thinking I said, 'And for ever is a long, long time.'

They both looked at me as if I was mad.

Trev said, 'What you on about, dafthead?'

They just didn't understand and it was no good trying to explain to them.

That's when I realized I was really missing Frankie.

When she came back, she lived at our house again for a few weeks while her mother decorated this new house she'd bought. Her mum and dad had broken up for good this time. She didn't say much but I knew she was upset. 'Grown-ups are so stupid,' was all she said. It made me wonder

if my mum and dad would break up and how I'd
feel about it. I didn't think they would, though.
They'd have no one to argue with. I was really
worried in case Frankie and me didn't get on like
we'd done before. But nothing was different. It
was like she'd never been away. When we met
again we didn't say 'Hello' or anything, like
other kids might. I'd known she was coming
but I'd gone down the garden in case anybody
might think I was keen to see her. She walked
down the garden towards me and said, 'I met a
conjuror in Belgium, d'you want me to show you
some tricks? Did you miss me? I'm pleased to see
you.'

I didn't know what to say, so I just shrugged
and said, 'What's the trick?'

She just smiled and tried to show me how
to make an egg disappear into your ear and then
reappear again. I tried, but I wasn't much of a
conjuror.

I thought it was important to tell her that I
was glad she was back but I didn't know how
to do it. Whenever I tried it out in my head, it
sounded stupid.

Then on my birthday I found a way to do
it that didn't embarrass me. The day before, I'd
been sitting on the swing in our back garden. I
was thinking how I didn't want my birthday to
be the same as it had been last year and the year
before. I just didn't want to get up in the morning, open a few presents, blow out eleven candles
and then go back to bed a year older. I wanted it

to be somehow different, but I didn't know how. My mum and dad were planting some flowers and arguing as usual.

'This has red petals.'

'No it doesn't.'

'Look at the picture on the cover.'

'They're all that colour.'

'No they're not.'

Frankie was trying to draw a picture of Sam but he wouldn't stay still long enough. It was really hot. I swung myself backwards and forwards on the swing, scuffing my shoes in the bare grass. I was quite bored but I wasn't miserable. With Frankie, even being bored seemed interesting. I tried to make myself just swing backwards but it was difficult to stop. As I was doing it I had this funny idea. I suppose I was thinking of my birthday and getting older.

I said to Frankie, 'Be funny if the years went backwards.'

'You mean, we got younger and younger instead of older.'

'Yeah. Started out at ninety then on your first birthday you'd be eighty-nine.'

'Before that you'd have to start off being dead.'

'Then you'd be ninety.'

'Or whatever age you were when you died.'

'Then eighty-nine.'

'And so on.'

'Everything would be back to front.'

'Like the things people say.'

'You'd say, like, "Wonder what I'll do when I grow young".'

'If you asked your mum a question and she didn't want to answer, like they do – like when you ask something like, where do babies come from? She'd say, "Time enough for that when you're younger." '

'If you were bald your hair would start growing again.'

'Then you'd get younger and younger until you went into hospital with your mum.'

'And got born.'

'Got dead.'

'Dead?'

'Well, you wouldn't be anywhere, would you? That's what being dead is.'

I laughed. I was quite proud of myself for thinking up the idea of living backwards. It would last us a long, long time that. We'd be adding to it for weeks.

Then Frankie said, 'You know you wanted your birthday to be different, Benbow?'

I nodded. She was going to come up with something. I tried to think how living your life backwards could make my birthday better.

'Well, that's what you can do tomorrow. Go backwards.'

I didn't understand. 'You can't really do that.'

She shook her head, annoyed that I hadn't caught on. 'No, no. Not get younger. Just do everything backwards.'

'Everything?'

I thought about it.

'People would think we were mad.'

'Who cares? You've got a lifetime living forwards, what difference will a day of backwards make? Might even catch on. Perhaps they'll have a National Living Backwards Day. Like Guy Fawkes Night or Hallowe'en.'

I thought a bit more.

'If you're too scared of what people will think, forget it.'

'Not scared,' I protested.

'Shall we do it?'

'We'll do it.'

So on my birthday for the whole day we did everything backwards. Everything.

We went to bed in our clothes and got up and put our pyjamas on, back to front. We walked backwards downstairs and had our suppers. We even talked backwards. So instead of saying, 'Pass the marmalade, please' or 'What a nice day it is today', we'd say, 'Please marmalade the pass' and 'Today is it day nice a what'. It was really difficult to start with but you got better with practice. Even Mum and Dad joined in.

Mum said, 'Breakfast after lawn cut the will you.'

But of course Dad had to argue.

'Wrong that got you.'

'Wrong that get not did I no.'

'Did you yes.'

'Not did I no.'

'Did you yes. Said you, "Breakfast after lawn

cut the will you," and it should have been, "Breakfast after lawn the cut you will." '

'I never. I said, "Breakfast after lawn cut you will."'

But they both laughed when Dad said, 'Kitchen the paint to have I lawn the cut can't I anyway.'

I thought if they talked backwards all the time perhaps they'd get on better.

At the end of the day we had breakfast and went to bed. They let us stay up till nearly midnight. It had been exhausting talking backwards all day. I climbed into bed. Sam was fast asleep. It had been a great day. And it was Frankie's idea that had made it. I could hear her in the bathroom. Then I thought of something I could do. I switched on the bedside light and tore a piece of paper out of an exercise book and wrote in capitals:

YOU MISSED I. HOUSE OUR TO BACK COME YOU'VE GLAD AM I.

I crept down the landing and laid the message on Frankie's pillow. When I switched off my light and slipped into my bed I wondered if I'd done the wrong thing. What if she told them at school. I could hear her voice saying, 'And d'you know what he did, he wrote me this really soppy note.' It would go all round the school. Everybody would laugh at me.

I heard her coming out of the bathroom. Her bedroom door closed. Downstairs I could hear Dad saying, 'Out cat the put just will I' and the sound of Mum laughing. Then a shaft of light crossed Sam's bed as the door opened. He woke up and raised his left hand, shielding his eyes. Frankie was in the doorway. I could only see the outline of her. Like a shadow. She didn't say anything for a time then she whispered, 'Too me.'

In the dark I was smiling. I thought that was funny because nobody would be able to see. Then she was gone, back to her room.

Sam said, 'Who was that?'

I didn't say anything. Sam was half asleep. His voice was thick.

'She's going home soon, isn't she? You can go back to your own room, then I'll be able to sleep.'

I thought for a minute and said, 'One you belt will I or Sam sleep to go you.'

Sam didn't answer. He was already asleep.

5

I ran panting up to our front gate. My mind had been so full of the night I'd first met Frankie, the fight with Big Halsey and my birthday when we'd done everything backwards that I hadn't noticed anything along the way. I'd run about a mile without realizing it.

Frankie was there before me. She was hardly out of breath.

'What kept you?' she asked.

I leaned on the gate, my head down, panting.

'I was thinking.'

'Thinking?'

'About when you came to our house. The first time.'

'The sad, lonely orphan.' She was smiling as she said it.

'Remember that time, on my birthday, when we did everything backwards?'

She was leaning with her back to the gate, her elbows on it, looking out into the street.

'Benbow,' she said, 'I've been thinking. It might be a good idea to go in for that play.'

I looked at her.

'Might be fun,' she said.

I couldn't believe what I was hearing. 'What

with Maitland, Betty Mallard and them? You must be joking.'

'It would be different. Better than playing football all the time. You never know, you might be good at it. Until you try something you never know what you're good at.'

'I hate acting.'

'Why?'

'I just do,' I said. 'Alan Maitland and that mob. Stupid.'

'Stupid? That's your favourite word, isn't it? Whenever you can't understand anything you say it's stupid.'

'I know that acting's stupid.'

She looked at me from under her eyebrows then swung off the gate.

'Well,' she said, 'I might try it.'

She sauntered off without saying goodbye.

I wondered what I'd said.

'What about the game? The replay's a week on Friday.'

She waved without looking over her shoulder.

Like always, I watched her until she'd disappeared round the corner into Halifax Road. She never looked round once. I knew she wouldn't even think about it. If it had been me I would have been thinking – It'll look good if I don't look round. But I'd have had to force myself. It wouldn't have been natural. With Frankie you felt that even if she was walking away to war or to be executed or something she still wouldn't have looked back.

When I reached our front door Sam was crouched in the porch shivering and looking fed up. Sam was the best person in the world at looking fed up. If there'd been Olympic medals for looking fed up he'd have taken the gold.

'There's no one in,' he said.

I rang the bell. There was no answer.

'I've done that,' he said.

I rattled on the letter box.

'I've done that,' he said.

I peered through. It was funny being able to see the inside of our house when it was empty. That's how it would look all the time when I wasn't there. I'd sometimes think about that in school; think about our house being there all empty. I sometimes used to think I'd come home and there'd be nobody there, ever. That they'd gone away, all of them and I'd never see them again.

I could see the letters on the hall table and past them to the kitchen. I could hear the grandfather clock ticking.

'Mum,' I shouted, and then louder still, 'Mum!'

'I've done that,' said Sam.

I gave him a push, 'Oh you, you've done everything.'

He started snivelling.

He cried about everything, did Sam. Once he started he'd go on and on, making things worse.

'I'm cold,' he snivelled.

'I'm cold, too, but I'm not crying about it.'

Then he really started. One of his long moans. He imagined everything getting worse and worse. 'We'll never get in the house now. They're never coming back. They've left us. Maybe they're both dead. They'll put us in a home or we'll die out here in the cold.'

'If you're going to die, I wish you'd hurry up and get on with it and give us a bit of peace.' I held my fist under his nose. He looked at it seriously for a minute and then started crying louder than before.

'There's a spare key,' I said. 'You're not supposed to know about it so don't tell anybody, all right?'

As soon as he realized there might be something that he shouldn't be doing, he got interested and stopped crying.

I dug the key out of the earth in the third plant pot along the wall. It was wrapped in greaseproof paper. I unlocked the door and we went in.

'Put the key back,' I told him.

Being in the house on my own reminded me of that film, the one where this young girl goes home and arms keep coming out of the walls and try to strangle her. I walked in the middle of the hall well away from the walls.

I shouted out 'Mum' once more, even though I knew she wouldn't be there. Of course she didn't answer.

Sam came in. He'd found something else to moan about now.

'I'm hungry.'

I decided to scare him. I said in a low whisper, 'They say that in some houses the arms of the long dead still lie in the wall and if you cry they come out suddenly and strangle you.'

He looked round nervously at the walls. His eyes were wide open.

'Give over messing about,' he said.

'Stop crying then.'

He bit his lip. I could tell I'd scared him but I knew it wouldn't last long.

On the kitchen table was a tray with a teapot, milk, sugar, biscuits and lardy cakes. Leaning against the teapot was a note. I didn't need to read it. I knew what it would say. 'I've had to stay on late for rehearsals. Make Grandad his pot of tea and have a cake to keep you going.'

I'd had hundreds of notes like that. I hated plays and acting. As far as I was concerned, plays meant your mum coming in late and having to make your own tea. Or, when I was little, being woken up to be given a goodnight kiss in the middle of the night.

I poured Sam a glass of milk. He took a biscuit and went upstairs to read his *Beano*.

I looked round the kitchen. There was something wrong. But I didn't know what it was. It was like something itching at the back of my mind but I couldn't work out what it was. Like when you look at a photograph and it's all blurred. Or when you try to remember someone's name. It's on the tip of your tongue but no matter how hard you try it won't come back to you.

I lit the gas under the kettle. The key turned in the front door. That would be her.

'Mum,' I shouted.

Grandad came into the kitchen with the evening paper under his arm.

'Where's your Mum?'

'She's out, Grandad. She's still at that rehearsal.'

'I thought I heard you talking to her.'

'I thought she'd just come in.'

Grandad turned towards the front door.

'Has she just come in?' he said.

'No,' I said. 'I thought it was her but it was you who just came in.'

But Grandad hadn't heard me. He'd gone out into the hall. He came back.

'No, it's not your mum. It was me who just came in. You must have thought it was your mum. She must be still out at that rehearsal. It gets longer every week.'

'Mum's rehearsal?'

'The queue at the post office. I was near half an hour in that queue.'

It was quite tiring talking to Grandad sometimes. Especially as you had to shout a lot of the time.

The kettle whistled.

His eyes lit up as he heard it and he raised his finger.

'That'll be her at the door now. She must have forgotten her key.'

'It's the kettle, Grandad.'

But he'd gone again. He came back in shaking his head.

'No, there's no one there.'

'It was the kettle, Grandad.'

'Can't understand it. Unless it was the kettle. That's what it was. The kettle whistling. You know they should have one just for stamps.'

I poured the boiling water into the teapot.

'What?' I said. I didn't know what he was on about.

'At the post office. They should have a queue for stamps. Exclusive for stamps.'

'I'm making a pot of tea, Grandad.'

'Where's your mum then?'

'She's still rehearsing. I'll bring it through into the greenhouse. You always have it in there, don't you, Grandad?'

He was standing by the kitchen window, trying to read the paper without using his glasses. He held it up and at arm's length. He looked up at me and smiled.

'Tell you what, Benbow, why don't we have a cup of tea?'

'I'm making it now.'

'Are you making it?'

'I'm making it now.'

'I don't want it here, you know. I want it in the greenhouse. I always have it there. Warm in there. I've got the paper. You can read me a bit. I can't see it so well now. They print it so small, you see. They used to print them much bigger.'

'It's your eyesight, Grandad. It's not the paper.'

'Unless it's my eyesight.'

'Mum's left some biscuits.'

'You what? No, she's gone to a rehearsal. Don't ask me where. Hasn't she left you a note?'

He shuffled through towards the greenhouse. Over his shoulder he shouted, 'Bring us a couple of biscuits. She usually has a few lying around.'

I couldn't resist eating one of the lardy cakes. I put a couple of ginger biscuits on his plate. He liked ginger biscuits. He'd dip them in his tea till they were soggy and started to bend. I was so hungry I stuffed a lardy cake into my mouth in one go. I put Mum's note on the table without bothering to read it and carried the tray through into the greenhouse. It wasn't really a greenhouse, just a room made of glass that led off the kitchen. Mum called it a conservatory. She kept big green plants in it. Dad grew tomatoes. It was him that called it a greenhouse. I liked the warm of it and the smell of the tomatoes.

Grandad was sitting in his easy chair with the paper across his lap. He'd fallen asleep. I put the tin tray down with a clang on the wooden table next to his chair. He woke up with a start.

'It's only me, Grandad.'

'Is that you? How do, Sam?'

'It's Ben,' I said.

'That's right,' said Grandad.

'I've brought your tea.'

'Have you brought the tea?'

I poured out the tea and put it on the table near him. Though there was no sun it was really warm in the greenhouse. Even so, Grandad was still wearing his old blue suit with a waistcoat and tie.

'That's right, put it on the table,' said Grandad.

He picked up the cup and poured the tea into his saucer, blew on it and drank it. Mum hated it when he did that. It didn't bother me, though. He looked at the plate.

'I thought I was going to have a lardy cake. She usually leaves me a lardy cake. I like your mum's lardy cakes.'

I opened my mouth and pointed. 'I had it, Grandad. I thought you liked the ginger.

'That's right,' he said, 'you have the ginger if you want it.'

Suddenly he laughed and pointed at his right leg. 'I could kick in those days, by heck I could kick a ball. Kick it further than your eyesight could see.'

He rolled up his trouser. His leg was thin and white.

'That leg,' he said, 'that leg scored the penalty that put Everton out of the Cup.' We both stared at it in silence. He rolled up his other trouser leg. There was a long white scar down the shin.

'And that leg scored the goal against Arsenal that took us to the Final.'

He sat looking out at the garden for a moment. Then he smiled.

'Did I never tell you how Arsenal came for me? Did I never tell you that story?'

'No, Grandad,' I lied. He loved telling that story.

'Fetch me suitcase.'

I knew which one he meant. He kept it under his bed. I brought it for him.

'It's under the bed in my bedroom . . . Oh, you've got it. Open it up.'

I opened it. It smelled of must and was full of photographs, programmes and yellowing newspapers.

'Let's have a look.'

He took the pile of papers from me and began shuffling through them.

'Here we are. That's me.'

He handed me a faded photograph. It showed a football team lined up with their arms folded.

'See if you can tell which is me.'

I looked through the line of figures. It was difficult to tell. I pointed at a smallish figure with hair combed straight back and baggy shorts down to his knees.

'Is that you, Grandad?'

He peered at it. 'No, that's not me.' He looked closer. 'Is it?'

He ran his finger along the figures.

'There I am.'

He was on the back row. A small, smiling young man with a centre parting and a moustache. It was hard to believe that could be Grandad. I wondered if I'd ever be as old as he was.

'Grand side was that. Best Town ever had. We got to the Final that year. FA Cup Final. Best season they ever had. Two year previous they'd been in the Third Division North. Ended up near getting promoted to the First. Where are they now?'

'They're not in the League at all, Grandad. They went bankrupt three years ago.'

'See him?' He pointed to the figure I thought had been Grandad.

'That was my best pal, Scrapper Holloway. Best winger ever ran across Grace Park in shorts, I'll tell you. Better than Matthews. I was at school with him. I was at Waverley Street with him. He could make a ball talk, could Scrapper; make it sit up and say Hello. Would have played for England, no question. It was a joy to be on the same field with him. Got killed in the war. That Hitler, he had a lot to answer for. 'Course it were a different game in them days. Twelve pound a week. Not like now. Money's spoiled the game. No wonder they went bankrupt. Greed, you see. We didn't have no training them days. Just used to run round the pitch. They wouldn't let you see a ball during the week. Not till the Saturday. Their thinking was, if you was deprived of the ball all week you'd be hungry for it come Saturday.'

He poured out some more tea and drank it.

'Aye.' He took up an old *Echo*. On the front

73

page was a photo of Grandad with both arms folded, staring straight at the camera. Underneath it said in big letters,

Arsenal Pursue Town's Benbow

'Arsenal were after me. They must have had me watched. Our managing director come to see me. Arkwright come to see me. Begged me. Begged me not to go. Came to our house in his big car. Nobody had a car in Dacey Street in them days. Aye, Mr Arkwright. Owned the milling firm in Netherton. He came into our kitchen. Took his hat off. Me mam didn't know where to put herself. She'd never had a man who owned a car in the house before. Offered him a cup of tea. I didn't like him. He didn't look to me like a man you could trust. Three years I'd been with Town and he'd never spoken to me till then. Not a word. He took me out to dinner. Took me to a restaurant in Mill Street. Pleaded with me. Pleaded with me to stay. "Arthur," he said, "we've got Everton in the sixth round at home. And we can beat them, Arthur. I know we can beat them. But we need you. Without you we don't stand a chance."

'I said, "Mr Arkwright," I said, "you shouldn't have wasted your money taking me out to eat. The Town gave me my first chance. I'd have been in the mill, else. They did the right thing by me so I'll do the right thing by them. I know what's right, Mr Arkwright."

'Well, he stood up in the middle of that fine

restaurant in front of all them fine people and he shook my hand.

'"You've done the right thing, Benbow," he said, "I won't forget this."

'When Arsenal got in touch I told them straight, I weren't interested. And he were right. He were right, were Mr Arkwright. We knocked Everton out. We beat them down here. I got the winner with a penalty. There were fifty thousand in Grace Park. They went mad. When we came off, Mr Arkwright was waiting for us. Shook hands with every man jack. He said to me, "If I had my way, Benbow, this town would put up a statue to you."'

I was shuffling through the papers.

'I can't find anything about you at Wembley, Grandad.'

'That's another story, lad. In the semi-final who should we draw but the Arsenal; Arsenal at Bramall Lane. They were *the* big club in them days. The papers had written us off before we'd walked on the field. I thought to myself, I thought, I'll show 'em. We were drawing nil-nil. Five minutes to go and Scrapper put me through. The ball was halfway between me and Barney Copplestone, their centre-half. It was what they call a hospital pass. I just got there first then I heard my leg crack. Double fracture. My shin bone was sticking out through my sock. I heard the crowd roaring and I knew we'd be at Wembley. But they'd be going without me. I was twenty-two. I never played again. I don't know, maybe it was the doctor at the hospital did something wrong. They said I should have made a fuss. Got compensation. But I was never one to make a fuss about anything. Town won the cup. Then they got in the First Division for a couple of seasons. That's when they built the new stadium. Left Grace Park. Arkwright put a few quid in his pocket over that I can tell you. It were a nice ground were Grace Park. I've seen thirty thousand in there regular. It were a good ground to me. It suited. That was my last game, was that. They never came to see me. That Mr Arkwright, I never spoke to him after that. I thought – aye, I thought, you were quick enough to put your hat on and come out to see me in your big flashy car and take me out for a bite when you wanted something, weren't you, Mr High and Mighty Arkwright? But it's a different tale now. They sent me a letter with twenty pounds in. Twenty pounds! I sent it back. I didn't want their money. Never went back after that. Never!'

He sat there in silence for a few moments, gazing out of the window. I looked through the newspapers. There was a big photograph of Grandad kicking a ball.

'Can I keep this one, Grandad?'

'What for?'

'I don't know. Just to keep.'

He took all the cuttings and folded them. Put them back in the suitcase. 'You'll have 'em all when I'm gone,' he said.

Sam came bursting in eating a piece of bread and jam. The jam was all round his mouth. My dad was in the hall wearing a mackintosh.

Grandad said, 'Hello, Ben.'

'It's Sam,' said Sam.

'That's right,' said Grandad.

'Everything all right?' shouted Dad from the hall. He hung his coat up and came into the greenhouse. 'Is he in here then?' he looked round.

I thought he was talking about me. Then Dad turned towards me.

'I thought he'd be in here with you. Have you put him to bed?'

I felt the flesh shrinking on the back of my neck and the hairs standing up. Standing up and crawling.

'Is that what your mum said in her note, to put Andrew to bed?' asked Dad.

Andrew! That's what had been worrying me; what had been at the back of my mind all that time. I knew there was something.

I heard my dad going up the stairs. I crept towards the greenhouse door that led into the back garden.

Upstairs, I heard my dad going from room to room. 'Well, where is he then?' he shouted.

It was a good question. I opened the door.

'Where you off to?' asked Grandad.

'I've got to go somewhere,' I said. I closed the door silently.

Dad dashed in. 'Where's Andrew? You haven't left him, have you?'

But I didn't wait to answer. I was off and down our road as fast as I could go. Running towards Grace Park.

6

As fast as I could, I ran towards Grace Park. All the way there I was thinking about Baby Andrew. Terrible pictures kept coming into my mind. I tried to shake them off, to make my mind blank, but no matter what I did they kept coming back. There was Baby Andrew in his pram where I had left him, cold and crying. Baby Andrew being taken away by an old woman. Baby Andrew being tipped into an ash pit by some lads in leather jackets. And worst of all, Baby Andrew lying on the ground, dead. When I imagined this I couldn't help crying out aloud, 'It'll be my fault.' There was nobody about in the streets to hear me. Even if there had been I wouldn't have cared. That's how worried I was.

Baby Andrew. I'd never thought much about him before. He was just somebody who was about the place, like Sam or Grandad. Just a baby who dribbled his food or sometimes kept you awake with his crying. Quite a lot of the time I'd thought he was just a nuisance, especially when I had to look after him. and I wanted to be doing something else. But when I thought he might be dead, that I'd never see him again, I began to think he wasn't such a bad baby after all, as babies go.

I remembered something that Frankie had once said to me, just after she'd come back from Belgium. She'd said that all the things you dreaded and all the things you wanted would eventually happen to you. It depended which was stronger, your dread or your want. I thought about that again now. I thought, if I could see Baby Andrew smiling and happy in his pram exactly as I'd left him then that's what would happen. But I couldn't see him. I could make myself think it but I couldn't make myself *see* him, no matter how hard I tried. Then the picture of him lying dead on the floor came creeping back into my mind. The dread was winning. It really frightened me.

I turned into Leamington Road. The lights were going on in front rooms. It had never seemed such a distance from our house to Grace Park before. I thought if I counted the houses it would take my mind off Baby Andrew; make the time pass more quickly. A lady pulled the curtains across. Just before they closed I saw a man and two little girls sitting down to tea. I only saw them for an instant and then they were gone. I thought it was all right for them. They hadn't left their baby brother in the park to die. For them it was just another ordinary day. I thought there must have been times when I'd been sitting down to tea on an ordinary day and somebody else might have been going down the street outside. Somebody who'd done something terrible. And I hadn't worried about them so why should anybody care about me now?

As I reached the outskirts of Grace Park I saw something that made me stop in my tracks. Parked half on the road and half on the pavement was a police car with its blue light flashing. A policewoman was sitting in the back seat. Behind the car and further off were two larger lorries. Four men in donkey jackets and yellow helmets were unloading something heavy off the back of the lorries. They were too far off for me to see what it was. I wondered if it had anything to do with Baby Andrew. Perhaps they were looking for me. I started creeping towards the wood across the patch of open ground. The back door of the police car opened and the policewoman got out. I stopped dead still. She had her back to me. I crept as quietly and slowly as I could in the direction of the trees. Any moment, I expected her to turn round and spot me. But she didn't and I reached the safety of the trees. Once there I felt safe and ran towards where I'd left the pram, dodging in and out of the trees. It was really dark in the wood. I kept wishing Frankie was with me. She would have known what to do. I tried to imagine what she would have said, what she would have done. She'd have probably walked straight up to the policewoman and asked her straight out what was going on. Perhaps that would have been the sensible thing to do. But I couldn't bring myself to do it. I'd somehow got it into my head that if I asked someone, the news would be bad. Anyway, it was too late now. Perhaps everything would turn out all right but, on the other hand, why were the police there at all? Nobody but us used Grace Park. They wouldn't have been there unless something had happened.

What about those men in the lorries, what were they doing? Perhaps they were part of a search party. They were making a search for the body. Like that time when Pauline Woodhead had disappeared. It was in all the papers. I'd been taking an exam in the school hall. I'd answered all the questions I could, and had lifted my head to look out of the window. There they were, on the waste ground, out beyond the football and cricket pitches; men and women walking slowly in a long straggling line all looking at the ground. I didn't know what they were up to at first and then I realized that they must be searching for Pauline Woodhead's body. But they never found her because she wasn't dead at all. She'd only run away from home. She'd met this boy from another school on the weekend trip we took to Boulogne. She was going to meet him in London. But she'd only got as far as Crewe when she ran out of money and decided to come home again.

As I emerged from the wood and into the open field it became a little lighter. It was funny being there on my own and at night. I looked towards the place where I'd left the pram. I couldn't see anything. But it was quite dark. I hurried towards the spot. I kept repeating to myself, 'Please God, let it be there. Please God, I'll do anything, only let Baby Andrew be alive.'

I stopped by the short poles we used for goal posts. I looked round but there was no sign of the pram. I looked again. Even though I was convinced I was in the right place I persuaded myself that I might be wrong. Perhaps I'd wheeled it to the other side of the ground or maybe Sam or Trev had moved it and I hadn't noticed. My heart was beating fast and my mouth was dry. I raced round the edge of the ground, looking to right and left. Halfway round I tripped over something hard and bulky, scraping my shins. For a moment I thought it was the pram, but it was only a rusty old fridge that someone had thrown out. I limped round the rest of the field. My leg was bleeding and my trousers were torn. Suppose he had been taken? I'd never be able to go home again. My mum would never forgive me. If I was to run away like Pauline Woodhead they'd think *I* was dead too. Then when I came back again they'd be so relieved I was still alive that they'd forgive me. Or perhaps I could have a bad accident.

As I was running I was crying out, 'Andrew, Andrew, where are you? It's me, Benbow.' I didn't care who heard any more. I knew that even if he heard me he wouldn't be able to answer, but I kept shouting just the same.

Then I heard a sound. It sounded like squealing. It was from somewhere near the goal posts. Near where I'd started. Perhaps that was him. It was a terrible noise. Almost like an animal in pain. It made me shiver. I wrapped my arms round myself and crept slowly towards the sound not wanting to see what I might find there. Then I saw it. A piece of an old tin advert. As the wind blew, it scraped against a broken piece of the wall. I let my breath out in relief and looked down at the ground. There were two lines in the grass. The wheels of the pram. That proved I was in the right place. It was hard to see in the half light but the tracks led away towards the wood. That's where they must have taken him. They? Who were they? Perhaps there was only one of them. Whoever they were, they'd wheeled Andrew away.

The torch beam hit me full in the face and a man's voice said, 'What are you doing here?'

I held my hand up to my eyes but I was dazzled by the torch light.

'Well?' said the voice. The torch light left my face and travelled slowly down my body. I could see a shadowy figure about ten yards away. I shivered.

'I asked you a question,' said the man. 'I'm waiting for an answer.'

'I was looking for somebody.'

There were spots in front of my eyes from the torchlight.

The man walked towards me. 'I see,' he said. 'Who would that be?'

'Andrew,' I said. 'I'm looking for Andrew.'

'Andrew? Who's Andrew when he's at home?'

'He's my brother. My baby brother.'

'Your brother? What's he doing here?'

'I left him. I left him here.'

'Left him. Bit careless, wasn't it?'

I could see now that the man was a policeman. He took out a two-way radio and held it to the side of his face. A distorted crackling came out of the radio and then a voice.

'Does your mum know you're here?' The policeman asked.

'No. Yes,' I stuttered.

He spoke into the radio. 'I've got something interesting here. I'll be over. You were right. Down in the forest something stirred. Over and out.'

He put his hand on my shoulder. 'You do know you're not supposed to be here, don't you?' he said, and pushed me in the direction of the road.

I wondered if I was being arrested. Twenty minutes ago I'd been sitting with Grandad drinking tea, eating lardy cakes and listening to his stories. Now I was being arrested. I wished I knew what I was supposed to have done. What did the policeman mean when he said I wasn't supposed to be there? Grace Park was just an old abandoned ground. Nobody used it except us and a few old men who had allotments. It wasn't a proper park. Not like Sefton Park where you weren't allowed to play on the grass and they closed the gates at night. He couldn't be arresting me for that. It must be Andrew. If he'd been safe, the policeman would have told me about him. Something had happened to Andrew and they thought I'd done it. They were arresting me as a suspect. I started crying. I couldn't help it. Snot came down my nose. I wiped it off with my shirt sleeve and sniffed.

'Are you all right?' the policeman asked.

'Got a cold,' I said.

We came out of the woods into the clearing by the road. The police car was still there. It had its headlights on. Behind it, the men were still unloading something off the lorries. On the road, cars whistled by. I wondered if they saw me and wondered what I was being arrested for. I held my head up and tried to look defiant and proud.

'Stop wriggling,' said the policeman.

I looked up at him.

'Why aren't I supposed to be here anyway?'

He looked down at me then switched on his torch and shone it at a wooden notice.

'That's why,' he said.

The notice said:

THIS LAND HAS BEEN ACQUIRED BY THOMAS ARKWRIGHT AND SONS.

'Can you read?'

'Yes.'

'What does it say?'

I read it aloud.

'And the rest.'

'TRESPASSERS WILL BE PROSECUTED. BY ORDER A. E. BRAITHWAITE, TOWN CLERK.'

The policeman switched off the torch and pushed me towards the car.

'You're a trespasser,' he said flatly.

At the car the policewoman was standing by the open front door. Messages were still crackling through the phone.

'I was just going to leave when you came through,' she said.

There was a huge crash as another bundle was hurled off the lorry. The three of us looked round.

'Take it easy,' said one of the men. A transistor radio was blasting out pop music.

The policeman took his hand off my shoulder.

'I think we may have the answer to our little problem, my dear.'

He said it in a jokey French accent. The policewoman didn't laugh. He opened the back door of the car and pushed me towards it. Lying on the back seat wrapped in white blankets was a bald baby with his eyes wide open, goggling. Baby Andrew. I'd never been so pleased to see anyone in my whole life.

'Andrew,' I said and picked him up.

He gurgled and waved his fists at me. He was pleased to see me, too.

'Looks like you know one another,' said the policewoman. 'Get in.'

I sat in the back seat with Andrew on my knee. The policeman collapsed the pram and put it in the boot.

The policewoman sat in the passenger seat. She leaned over the back of the seat and looked at me. She'd taken her hat off. Her hair was blonde, streaked with brown. She looked different without her police hat on. Just like an ordinary woman.

'How come you left him?' she asked.

Baby Andrew had fallen asleep.

'We were playing football. My grandad asked me to take him to our house. I forgot.'

'Careless,' she said.

The policeman started the car.

'How did you find him?' I asked.

'The men were measuring the park. They told us.'

The car turned towards the road.

'Where to?' asked the policeman.

I told him our address.

'Will my mum have to know?'

'Of course she'll have to know. You can't go leaving babies all over the shop and keep it secret. What d'you think this is, Disneyland? Anyway, it's in the book now. There's an official report. Your name's in the book, my son. How do we know it's yours for a start?'

I thought, I'd hardly be walking round a wood at night on the off chance that I might find an abandoned baby. But I didn't say anything. We went past the Cottage Hospital and the school playing fields. We'd be home soon. I wondered if the blue light was flashing. I sank into the seat. I wasn't looking forward to facing Dad. I wondered if my mum would be home by now. I started playing this game. Whenever something bad happens I start imagining what it would be like if it was ten times worse. It makes things better. I imagined myself standing at our front door with the cold body of Andrew in my arms and two policemen standing behind me looking solemn. My mum would come to the door rubbing her hands on her pinafore.

'Yes?' she'd say.

The policemen would take off their hats.

'I'm afraid we've got some terrible news.'

I shook my head. I couldn't see any further. I couldn't imagine how Mum would react. I tickled Andrew under the chin.

'You're alive aren't you, Andrew?'

Andrew didn't care. He was fast asleep.

The car pulled into our street and stopped outside our house.

Things could be worse, I thought, and got out of the car.

7

'What happened next?' asked Frankie.

It was a fortnight later and the six of us were walking down Scarisbrick New Road towards Grace Park. It was the big day. The final replay of the England-Brazil game. The game that was going to go on for ever if need be. It was the first time I'd been back to Grace Park since I'd lost Baby Andrew. John Stokes and Trev were walking up ahead, arguing and punching each other; Sam was trailing behind, chanting 'Brazil, Brazil' and Carlton, Frankie and me were walking together. I'd been telling them what had happened the day I'd lost Baby Andrew.

'When my mum saw the police she thought something terrible must have happened. As soon as she saw Andrew was safe she started crying and put her arms round us both. Then she shouted at me and belted me. Then she started crying all over again.'

'My mum did that the time we went cycling to see this church in Ormskirk,' said Carlton. 'I turned right instead of left and ended up in this sewage works at Brockton. They rode on for a mile before they noticed I wasn't following. I was only eight.'

'Your mum cried?' I couldn't imagine Carlton's mum crying. She was a really big woman with a loud voice.

'No, she didn't cry, she just belted me,' said Carlton.

Frankie said, 'Were you scared in there in Grace Park on your own at night?'

Just thinking about it made me go cold.

'I wasn't scared of the dark. I was scared something might have happened to Baby Andrew.'

'Yah, you liar,' said Carlton, 'I bet you cried your eyes out.'

'Stupid,' I said, ''course I didn't.'

Frankie looked at me. That way she had. As if she was looking right through you. But I wasn't going to admit I'd cried in front of Carlton. It would have been all over the school next day.

We'd reached the outskirts of the park. Trev punted the ball into the air and everybody except me and Frankie piled after it shouting and whooping.

She looked at me. 'What d'you think all those lorries were doing there? What were they unloading?'

I shrugged my shoulders.

We soon found out.

At the point where we usually walked through the trees was a wall of wire netting ten feet high. We all stood looking at it, not saying anything, as though if we stared long enough it would suddenly disappear. But it didn't.

Trev and Carlton started running along it in

different directions but it was soon obvious that the whole park had been fenced in.

'Look at this,' shouted John Stokes.

He was standing in front of a big sign. It was like the one the policeman had made me read, only four times bigger.

Carlton read it out loud.

THIS LAND HAS BEEN ACQUIRED BY THOMAS ARKWRIGHT AND SONS FOR REDEVELOPMENT AS A SHOPPING MALL. UNITS, SHOPS AND FACTORY SITES AVAILABLE. TRESPASSERS WILL BE PROSECUTED. BEWARE GUARD DOGS PATROLLING.

'What's prosecuted?' asked Sam.

'It means you get shot if you go in,' said Carlton.

Sam's eyes went wide and he started to back away. He was a terrible coward.

Trev suddenly gave a scream. 'Look out,' he shouted, 'here comes the guard with a gun.'

Everybody except Frankie, Trev and me dived for cover. Sam was crying.

But there was nobody there.

Trev laughed. 'Only kidding,' he said.

They all wandered back again.

'They don't shoot you,' said Frankie. 'They're not allowed.'

'No, they just have dogs that eat you alive,' said Trev.

'Dogs! I'm not scared of dogs,' said Carlton. 'There's not a dog alive that can scare me.'

'You would be of these dogs. They're trained to kill,' said John Stokes. 'I saw it on the telly.'

'Wouldn't bother me,' said Carlton.

'I know what Carlton would do,' said John Stokes, 'he'd set his mum on them. She'd scare 'em off.'

'She'd eat them alive.'

'Wouldn't need to. They'd only have to look at her. They'd drop dead with fright.'

Trev started to pretend he was a dog that had just seen Carlton's mum. He stuck out his tongue and made his hands look like paws.

'Aaaah,' he screamed, 'it's Carlton's mum. Help!'

And he lay on his back trembling with fear, both arms stretched out.

John Stokes always copied whatever anybody else did. He lay down next to Trev.

'I surrender, I surrender,' he shouted.

Carlton pretended not to notice but you could tell he was mad. He stuck his finger into his forehead. 'You're mental, you lot.'

Frankie was standing by a bigger notice.

It was a picture of what the new shopping mall would look like. There was a big red brick shop like a warehouse and hundreds of cars parked. Lots of men, women and children were walking from the shop with big parcels and wire prams looking happy and smiling about all the things they'd bought. You couldn't recognize Grace Park any more.

'Where's the pitch gone?' said John Stokes.

We stared at the picture. It was hard to work out where everything was.

'It'll be under the baked beans counter,' said Trev.

Everybody laughed. But he was probably right.

'It's not funny,' I said. It made me sad to think that the spot where Grandad had scored that penalty would be hidden for ever. That people would be walking round there doing their shopping not knowing what had happened there a long time ago. I didn't think Grandad would be too pleased when he found out. Maybe it would be best not to tell him.

We were all silent for a long time.

Then Carlton said, 'Well, that's it, isn't it? That's the end.'

'What you mean, the end?' said Trev.

'We can't play here, can we? Not with that net up, not with all those buildings.'

'No, I suppose not.'

We all started to walk away.

Frankie looked at us, her eyes blazing. 'Is that all you can say? Are you going to give up just like that? It's not their field. It's ours.'

'What can we do?' said Carlton.

I thought about the Final we were supposed to be playing; the years we'd been coming to Grace Park. And before us all those other kids. It was our field. We hadn't paid for it but it was ours just the same. Why should anybody be allowed to stop us just because they had a lot of money?

'Frankie's right, it is our field.'

'Oh yeah,' said Carlton 'and how are we supposed to play football when there's a dirty great building there? Don't be daft.'

'There's no building there now. It'll take them months, maybe years to build it.'

'Pardon me, but perhaps you haven't noticed,' said Carlton, being very sarcastic, 'there's a dirty great fence in the way. What are we supposed to do about that?'

'Climb over it,' said Trev.

'Climb . . .'

'Unless you're scared.'

'What about the dogs?'

'What dogs?'

'On the other side. Can't you read? It says, dogs patrolling.'

'They always say that. If there'd been dogs there they'd have heard us by now. It's to scare off cowards like you.'

'Who are you calling a coward?' said Carlton.

'You,' said Trev. 'I can't see anybody else here.'

'Yeah, well who jumped in the canal that time? You didn't.'

This was true. Carlton had jumped off Brook Bridge into the canal one summer day two years ago and broken his ankle. He'd lived off this ever since. It was like a badge of courage he wore. He was always bringing it up.

'You didn't jump, you fell. Anyway, what a

stupid thing to do. Jump into a canal and break your ankle for nothing. Takes a loonie to do that.'

'I bleeding well jumped.'

'You fell. Benbow pushed you.'

They faced each other, breathing hard.

Frankie said, 'For God's sake, if you're going to fight I'm going home. I was getting bored with this football match anyway. I only came because it was the last one.'

I looked at her. She leaned against the fence and put her hands in the pockets of her jeans. Carlton and Trev didn't take any notice, they kept staring at one another, their fists clenched. Then suddenly Trev started barking like a dog. We all knew what he meant and so did Carlton. He went mad whenever anybody barked at him. It drove him crazy. But he pretended not to understand.

'What you barking at, stupid?' he said, going pink.

Trev just carried on barking and yapping.

Carlton pretended to laugh. 'Stupid you are. Suppose you think it's clever to go round barking. You'll go like it.'

'I'd rather be called stupid than be called after a dog.'

'Shurrup you,' said Carlton.

But it was true. Carlton had been named after a dog. In a weak moment one afternoon when we'd all been lying on Altcar Hill with our hands behind our necks staring at the white clouds streaming across the blue sky, we'd all started talking about our names and how we got called them. Like, although my name was Anthony Threlfall everybody called me Benbow which was my grandad's surname. When I'd first been born my grandad had said, 'He looks a real Benbow.' And it had stuck. Then Carlton came out with this story. His mum had a favourite dog that had died just before Carlton had been born. It had been run over by a drunken driver outside the sweet shop. She'd found it in the gutter the next morning, stiff and covered with blood. When Carlton was born she missed the dog so much that she called the new baby after him. Carlton. The minute he'd told us this I think he regretted it. He'd set up a lifetime of mickey-taking for himself. We never let him forget it. If you wanted to get at him, all you had to do was whistle or say something like, 'Carlton, here boy. Get that bone.' Frankie's was the best though. Whenever Carlton used to get on her nerves, making stupid remarks about the fact that she was only a girl and that all girls were stupid, she'd just say to him, 'Walkies'. That really drove him wild.

So as soon as Trev started barking Carlton went really mad. He stared at Trev. His face went pink and he was breathing hard. Trev just carried on barking.

Frankie came between them.

'It's no good fighting amongst ourselves. It's them we have to fight.' She pointed at the hoarding.

Carlton didn't look. 'He called me a coward,' he said, 'nobody calls me a coward. Take it back.'

Trev smiled at him. 'Woof woof,' he barked.

'I suppose you think you're funny, don't you?'

'Woof woof.'

'Since you like dogs so much, why don't you be first to climb over the fence then?'

That stopped Trev in his tracks. He couldn't refuse. He'd made the suggestion in the first place. Carlton relaxed. He'd caught Trev now. He could see that. He wasn't going to let go.

'What you scared of? There aren't any dogs, are there, anyway? You said. Why don't you go over to the pitch? If it's all clear we can carry on with the match.'

Trev looked at the fence, then back at us. We all stared at him. He saw there was no way out. He'd opened a trap door for himself and now he had to jump down it.

He made one feeble attempt to get out of it.

'The er . . . fence,' he said, 'I think it's electrocuted.'

Frankie was leaning on the fence. She held her hand up and clutched the mesh. Nothing happened.

'You'll be all right,' she said.

'Right,' said Trev, 'I'll er . . .' He looked at the fence. 'I'll need a leg up.' John Stokes and Carlton ran forward. They bent over and Trev put his feet on their shoulders. Then they slowly straightened. Trev put his fingers through the mesh.

'Nothing to it,' said Carlton.

He couldn't wait to see Trev fall off the fence or get eaten by a dog.

I wouldn't have liked to go over the fence even without the dogs. It swung about under the weight of Trev's body as he pulled himself up. He was almost at the top when there was the sound of barking and a large black dog came charging out of the trees. Trev gave a shout and fell backwards on top of John Stokes and Carlton knocking both of them off their feet. The dog ran up and down the fence, barking savagely. Even though there was a fence between us we backed away. Sam ran off into the trees and hid.

I could tell Trev was relieved that he hadn't had to go over. He'd been really scared a moment or two ago, now he could make jokes about it.

'I think it's Carlton's brother,' he said, pointing at the dog.

He'd be telling everybody at school all about it next week. I could just hear him.

'Anyway,' he'd say, 'I climb over this massive fence about twenty feet high. I'm just landing on the other side, right, when these three dirty big dogs come charging at me. I just managed to get to the fence when . . .'

And so it would go on, the lies getting bigger and bigger as time went by.

After a time the dog got tired of barking at us and trotted off back into the woods.

'That's it,' said John Stokes. 'No more world cups.'

Frankie looked at him.

'What d'you mean, that's it? Are you going to give up just like that? Without a fight?'

We stopped and looked round. She was standing with her hands on her hips. Her eyes were blazing.

'What can we do?' said Trev.

'What can you do?' shouted Frankie. 'There's a lot we can do. Doesn't it make you mad that they think they can come in here in a couple of lorries and take what's ours off us, just like that? It's not right. It's a principle. The park belongs to us. They just can't fence it off. Do they think they can frighten us off with a bit of fencing and a few measly dogs? It's our park. What have they ever done there? Nothing! We've played on it for years. Others before us. It's ours. Possession is three parts of the law.'

Nobody knew what she was talking about but it sounded good. We all murmured, 'Possession, yeah, right.' Frankie was always coming out with these phrases.

'What can we do?'

Frankie thought for a minute, her head down. We all looked at her. Then she looked up.

'We have to make a protest. Attract attention.'

'A protest?'

'People do it all the time. Get public sympathy. You all believe we have right on our side, don't you?'

We all murmured in agreement.

'How do we do that?' asked Trev.

'We do things.'

'What things?'

'All sorts of things,' said Frankie. 'People protest all the time. Like at Greenham Common.'

I'd never heard of Greenham Common but I wasn't going to let Frankie know.

'That's right, Greenham Common,' I said.

Trev said, 'I saw it on the telly. These people lying down in front of lots of tanks and lorries.'

'You could do that, for a start,' said Frankie.

'What would be the point of that?' asked Carlton. 'What's the point of getting run over by lorries? Wouldn't be much good at playing football then.'

'The idea is not to get run over. It's to stop the lorries coming in.'

'People do it,' said John Stokes. 'I saw Mrs Hewlett in our street. She was on the nine o'clock news. Sitting down in the middle of the road. It's called unarmed combat.'

'Peaceful Protest,' said Frankie.

'My mum would go mad if I did that. You get arrested for that,' said Carlton. 'What happens if the lorries don't stop? They might kill us.'

'You have to take that risk,' said Frankie. 'You have to get publicity. Attract attention. Get your name in the papers.'

'It's like being terrorists,' said Trev. 'They steal aeroplanes and make the pilot fly them where they want to go.'

'See you stealing an aeroplane,' said Carlton, laughing. 'Don't be stupid. How you going to get on one, for a start? You have to buy a ticket. It costs hundreds.'

'I didn't mean a plane. I mean steal something else.' He looked round. 'Like a lorry or something.'

'The JCB?' said Carlton.

'Yeah, come round at night and drive it.'

'Where you going to drive it?'

'I don't know. How should I know? You know, just drive it. To the Town Hall at midnight.' Trev was getting excited. He could see himself driving a JCB round town at midnight. 'In balaclavas, then leave it on the steps. On the steps of the Town Hall with a big sign saying 'Save our Football Pitch'.

'Then set fire to it,' said Carlton.

'Yeah, if you like,' said Trev. 'Set fire to it. Whoosh.' We all looked at him, very impressed. Trev took a breath. He was pleased with himself, too.

Frankie said, 'Can you drive?'

'Well, sort of.'

'What can you drive? What have you driven?'

'My dad's car.'

'You've driven your dad's car?'

'Well I've sat with him when he's driving. He sometimes lets me change gear.'

'So because you've sat next to your dad you think you can drive that thing.'

'I didn't mean me. I mean like anybody.'

He looked round. We all looked at one another.

Nobody could drive.

I wondered what my mum would do if she found out I'd set fire to a JCB on the Town

Hall steps. 'They'd never leave the key,' I said.

We were silent again.

Frankie said, 'We can't keep Grace Park open unless other people want it as well. What we ought to do before we start setting things on fire is to get as many signatures as we can and show them to somebody.'

'Who?'

'Well,' Frankie looked round. 'The man on the board. The Town Clerk.'

'What do we say? He'd never see us,' said Trev.

'We take a letter. A letter of protest.'

'Who'll write it?'

'We all will.'

'Who's got the best writing?'

Frankie said, 'My mum's got a typewriter. A typewriter would look better. Then we take it to the Town Clerk with this huge list of names. If *everybody* wants to save the Park he won't dare let it go ahead, will he?'

We all nodded.

John Stokes said, 'How do we get all them signatures?'

'We stand in the street with placards,' said Frankie.

'Where?'

'Where's the most crowded place? Where there are lots of people?'

'The High Street, near Sainsbury's. It's always crowded there. My mum takes me shopping sometimes. You can't move.'

'When?'

'When d'you get the most people?'

'Saturday. Saturday morning. That's when everybody goes shopping.'

Frankie smiled. 'Then that's when we'll do it. All bring a placard and some paper and a pen for the signatures to the High Street tomorrow morning.'

We walked back towards the road, talking about what we'd put on the placards and how big they'd be.

I walked home with Sam and John Stokes.

'When are we going to set the lorry on fire?' John Stokes asked.

'We're not doing that now.'

'No fire? Ah,' he said sadly, 'I like fires.'

8

A week later, on the first day of the holidays, the three of us stood together at the bottom of the steep row of steps gazing up. The Town Hall looked very big and I felt very small. If there had been six of us it might have felt better, but John Stokes hadn't even turned up with a placard to collect signatures the Saturday before, and Carlton had had to drop out after the row with his mum.

He'd arrived with the rest of us carrying a huge sheet that said:

IF YOU WANT TO SAVE GRACE PARK
TOOT YOUR HORN

'I saw the firemen do it when they were on strike and all these cars tooted their horns. It was great.'

We all agreed it sounded like a good idea.

Mine said:

PLAYING FIELDS BEFORE SHOPS

Trev's was written in red on a piece of hardboard nailed to a stick. It said:

THE GRACE PARK SIX
IF YOU'RE ON OUR SIDE SIGN OUR
PETITION AND SAVE GRACE PARK

Sam pointed out there were only five of us

but Trev said he couldn't change it because it would spoil the sign and that anyway John Stokes was with us in spirit, even if he wasn't there in person. I wasn't sure about that, but I didn't say anything.

Frankie had brought a long length of paper for all the signatures we were going to collect. I was hoping like mad my dad and mum wouldn't walk past, otherwise I'd be in dead trouble. I kept skulking in the doorway of Sainsbury's ready to dive inside if I spotted them, but the manager came out and told us not to block the doorway. We had to move a hundred yards down the road and stand outside a piece of derelict ground. I was dead embarrassed. I felt everybody was looking at me. Anyway, it was a complete waste of time. None of the cars tooted their horns and hardly anybody signed our petition. In the end Frankie started going up to people and asking them straight out in this really polite voice she has:

'Excuse me, I wonder if you'd be interested in signing our petition?'

She explained it was always best to be polite. People would let you burn their houses down if you asked them nicely and said please. But it didn't do any good this time. Some of the people listened patiently. Some even said they were sorry. But hardly any of them signed. The ones who did were kids at school. Like Marion Archard, who used to follow me round all over the place in Junior School and has a stutter, and Armitage who's in our class and really brainy. A couple of others signed as well; Mickey Travis and Euan Rose, but when we looked they'd only been messing about and had signed themselves as Margaret Thatcher and Donald Duck. That was typical of them.

Carlton got so fed up with being ignored that he started marching backwards and forwards on the zebra crossing. After a bit we all followed him. It was better than standing still and being ignored. A lot of the motorists started tooting their horns. At first I thought it was because they were on our side, but then I realized it was because they were mad at us for blocking the road. Then Sam started moaning because he was hungry and it began to rain.

We were just going to go home when a red car screamed to a halt and a big lady in a jogging suit climbed out shouting and waving her arms. She ran over to Carlton, tore the placard out of his hands, belted him across the ear and dragged him into the car. It was his mum.

So that Monday morning there were only four of us at the Town Hall; me, Frankie, Trev and Sam. Slowly we climbed the broad, granite steps. I could tell Trev was nervous because he kept whistling to try and show he didn't care. I kept hold of Sam's hand. I hadn't wanted him to come in case something went wrong. I hadn't wanted him to sign the letter either but he'd sulked so much I had to let him. He said he'd tell Mum if he couldn't sign his name so in the end we had to let him. Nine years of age and already a blackmailer!

After all the arguing he signed his name wrong. Instead of writing 'Sam' he put 'Slam'. Trev said it sounded more like a door shutting than a name. I didn't think it mattered, nobody would know it wasn't his real name. But Frankie said it was important so she typed the letter all over again and this time Sam got his name right.

At the top of the steps were two huge wooden doors.

'Who's got the letter?' asked Frankie.

I held up the big white envelope.

'I have,' I said.

Frankie pushed open one of the doors.

'Come on,' she said.

Trev hesitated. 'D'you think there's too many of us?' he said.

Frankie looked at him. 'What are you suggesting?'

Trev shrugged, 'Nothing. I just thought, you know, like four of us we might frighten him.'

'D'you want to take it in on your own while we wait here for you?'

'No,' said Trev quickly. 'I mean, well you know, I don't mind er . . .'

His voice trailed off.

'It's all or none,' said Frankie.

'That's what I meant,' said Trev, 'all or none.'

We nodded at each other emphatically.

'What do we do when we get inside?' I asked.

'We go straight up to his office, tell him why we're there and hand him the letter,' said Frankie.

She went inside and we marched through after

her. If I'd felt small before I felt even smaller once we were inside. There was a wide corridor in front of us leading to stone stairs with iron banisters that curved round a corner and out of sight. The floor was made of marble and there were red carpets. On the walls were rows of big oil paintings of cows standing in water.

A man in a peaked cap and a blue uniform with a leather strap over his shoulder was leaning on the desk, writing in a book. He looked up as we came in.

'What are you after?' he demanded.

He blew his nose into a big white handkerchief. When he blew, his face went very red.

Frankie took the letter off me and walked up to him.

'We want to see the Town Clerk,' she said.

'Oh yes,' said the man in uniform. He put his handkerchief in his pocket. There were purple veins on his nose. 'Have you an appointment?'

'No,' I said.

The man laughed in a sarcastic way and shook his head. 'You can't go up unless you've got an appointment.'

'But we have to see him,' I said. 'They're closing Grace Park.'

'Are they now? Well, you still have to have an appointment.'

'We wanted to give him a letter.'

'It's typed,' said Trev.

'I wrote my name on it,' said Sam.

The man looked at us all.

'Well, what can we do? I'll tell you what.' He took the letter. 'You let me have it and I'll make sure that he gets it.'

This wasn't at all what we wanted to do. When we'd written the letter I'd seen myself standing in front of a big desk handing it over to the Town Clerk. How did we know the man would give him our letter? He might put it in the basket or forget about it. I took our letter back.

I said, 'We wanted to give it to him ourselves. Explain all about it.'

The man frowned. He didn't like me taking the letter back.

'Couldn't we just go in? Just to give it him.'

He shook his head. 'It's more than my job's worth,' he said. 'Anyway you can't see him now, he's in a meeting.'

We looked at one another and moved away from the desk.

'What are we going to do? We'd better just give it to him, hadn't we?' said Trev.

'I'm hungry,' said Sam.

Frankie said, 'I think we ought to wait. We said we were going to hand it to him personally, didn't we? And that's what we ought to do.'

A man in a suit, carrying a brief case, strode past.

'Town Clerk in, Blenkinsopp?' he asked.

'Mr Braithwaite'll be along in a few moments, Sir Gerald. You go straight up, sir, he'll be along directly. You know where he lives.' He was smiling. He hadn't smiled like that when he'd talked to us.

The man skipped up the stairs.

We looked at one another, wondering what we should do. The envelope was still in my hand. I waved it at the man.

'Excuse me,' I said.

He didn't hear. I tapped him on the back. He turned.

'Excuse me. What about us?'

He looked down at me. 'I've told you he's in a meeting. He can't see anybody. Now do you want me to deliver the letter? If you do, give it here. If not, clear off because you're beginning to get on my wick.'

He leaned his face down towards me with his hand held out. His breath smelled of cigarettes. I looked round at the others. Frankie shrugged.

I handed him the letter.

'You will make sure he gets it, won't you?'

'I'll make sure he gets it. Now was there anything else? Because I'm a very busy man. If not, there's the door and if you want my advice you'll go out of it sharpish. Comprendez?'

I nodded. The man lifted the end of the desk and lowered it behind him. We all looked at him. He turned and jerked his head in the direction of the door and we went out.

We sat in a row at the top of the steps. I wasn't sure if we'd done the right thing. Sam scuffed in the dirt with his shoes.

I could tell Trev was relieved that it was over.

'Well, we did it,' he said. "I think we did the right thing giving the letter to that man.'

Frankie and me didn't say anything.

A big car drew up at the bottom of the steps. The chauffeur in a grey uniform opened the back door and a man with a moustache and very shiny hair got out, followed by a lady in a grey suit. The man raced up the steps. As he ran he kept his hand on his head. I wondered why he did that. The lady in the grey suit was having a job keeping up with him. They stopped to speak to somebody at the top of the steps.

I heard the lady saying, 'And then there's Sir Gerald Arkwright with the costings for the new development, Mr Braithwaite.'

We looked at one another when we heard his name.

'That's him, Mr Braithwaite, the Town Clerk,' said Trev.

I got up and walked over to him.

'Mr Braithwaite . . .' I said. But he didn't hear me and disappeared through the door and into the Town Hall.

Frankie said, 'That's Celia Braithwaite's dad. I remember him from Open Day. He made a speech.'

Celia Braithwaite was Head Girl at school. She was dead brainy and wore glasses.

'Come on,' I shouted and followed him. The

others ran after me. Mr Braithwaite was disappearing up the stairs. The lady was still running after him, talking as she went.

The doorman was writing in his book. We went over to him.

I said, 'Did you give him our letter?'

'What letter?' he said, without looking up. He scratched his ear with the pen.

'The letter we just gave you. Mr Braithwaite just went through. Did you give it him?'

He looked up. 'Oh, it's you lot.' He bent down and carried on writing. 'Hop it,' he said.

'Did you give it him? You promised you would,' said Frankie.

The man carried on writing. 'I gave it him.'

'What did he say?' I asked.

'Say?' said the man. 'He said he'd look into it.'

We stood there for a moment in silence, then Frankie said suddenly. 'Look at that kid scratching the mayor's car!'

The man looked up. 'What, where?' he shouted.

Frankie pointed through the doors. The man rushed out and ran down the steps.

As soon as he was gone, Frankie lifted up the wooden flap on the desk. She picked something out of a waste paper basket.

'Come on,' she said and raced up the steps.

We followed her.

'Did you really see somebody scratching the car?'

''Course not.'

'That man, he'll kill us when he finds out,' said Sam.

Frankie waved the letter. 'Well, he lied to us, didn't he? He never gave him our letter. He just put it in the waste paper basket.'

Where the staircase reached the landing and turned the corner, we stopped and looked up. There was no sign of Mr Braithwaite. We looked back and down the wide staircase. The doorman came rushing through the double doors and stared round him. He looked like a bull who's just been let out. We hid, crouching round the curve of the stairs. The man ran down one of the corridors beneath us.

We walked up the carpeted stairs to the next floor. There were corridors leading off in four directions with rows of office doors. There seemed to be hundreds of them. Mr Braithwaite could have been in any of them.

The lady in the grey suit walked towards us. I was going to hide but Frankie went straight up to her.

'Excuse me, we're looking for Mr Braithwaite's office,' she said in a loud, clear voice.

'Oh,' said the lady looking us up and down. 'Why would Mr Braithwaite want to see you?'

Frankie laughed. 'Oh,' she said, 'he's my dad. I've a message for him from Mum.'

'Oh,' said the lady. 'You must be Celia.'

'That's right, Celia,' said Frankie.

'He's always talking about you,' said the lady.

'All good, I hope,' said Frankie in a posh sort of voice.

The lady laughed. 'Fourth floor,' she said. 'Fourth door down from the lift. It's got his name on the door. Unless you want to take the stairs.'

'No, we'll take the lift,' said Frankie.

The lady smiled and walked round the corridor. I could hear her high heels clicking.

We all crowded into the lift. Frankie pushed the button marked fourth floor. I looked at Frankie with amazement and admiration.

She opened her eyes wide.

'Daddy will be pleased to see me,' she said.

We all broke out giggling and the lift whispered up to the fourth floor.

9

His name was written on a brass plate on the door, E. A. Braithwaite. We all stood outside, shuffling our feet and looking at one another. Nobody wanted to be the first to knock or to go in. It was like that time when Trev and me got sent to Mr Liversedge for putting our school dinners down a hole in the wall. We spent hours pushing each other towards the door and then backing away again because we were too scared to go in. Without thinking, I rubbed my shoes on the back of my trousers trying to get the dust off. Mr Braithwaite was the most important man I'd ever met. More important even than Mr Liversedge. Suddenly I felt I wanted to go to the toilet very badly.

'Go on then, knock,' said Trev, giving me a shove.

I pushed him back. 'I'm not knocking, man,' I said.

We both started giggling. Then Trev pushed Sam really hard and he banged up against the door with a crash. We both backed off laughing. Sam ran off and hid behind a white pillar.

Nobody came to the door. Frankie, who hadn't moved, said, 'Come on, they can't kill us.'

She knocked again. There was still no answer.

'Come on, man, there's nobody in,' said Trev. He started to walk away down the corridor.

'Wait!' said Frankie. Slowly she turned the handle and opened the door a few inches. We peered in over her shoulder. The office was empty.

'Come on,' said Frankie and we tiptoed in.

There was a desk with trays, a telephone inter-com and a typewriter. To the left was another door made of frosted glass. Frankie walked over to the desk and picked up a large blue diary. She started leafing through it.

Trev was hanging back near the door with Sam, ready to make a quick exit in case anybody came in.

'Put it down, they'll kill us if they catch us,' he said.

Through the door on the left I could see shadowy figures moving and voices talking. One of the shadows moved towards the door.

'Look out, someone's coming,' hissed Trev.

Frankie put the book down quickly and tiptoed back into the middle of the room. A woman with her hair piled on top wearing a white blouse and high heels came through the door. She was carrying a notebook and tapping her teeth with a silver Biro. She stopped tapping when she saw the four of us. She looked at us for a few seconds then closed the door behind her.

'What are you doing here?' she said.

Frankie said, 'We've come to see Mr Braithwaite.'

'It's about Grace Park.'

'They're not going to let us play there any more.'

'We've always played there.'

'We're a protest group.'

We were all speaking at once.

The woman looked at us and walked over to her desk. She turned over a few papers and looked in the drawers. I could tell that she was checking in case we'd pinched anything. She sat down and looked at us suspiciously.

'Does Mr Braithwaite know you're coming?'

'No,' said Trev.

'Yes,' said Frankie.

She looked from one to the other. 'You don't seem very sure,' she said.

'We're sure, all right,' said Frankie. 'Aren't we?'

'Yeah,' said Sam very loudly.

We all looked at him. It was unusual for Sam to say anything. He looked back at us with raised eyebrows and shrugged.

The woman picked up the blue diary and turned the pages.

'Have you an appointment?' she asked.

'Oh yes,' said Frankie. She sounded so confident I almost believed her myself.

The girl looked at Sam.

'Are *you* sure?'

Sam looked round at us. Frankie gave a tiny

encouraging nod of her head. Sam nodded his head vigorously.

Trev was still standing by the half open door.

'Are you with them?' the woman asked him.

Trev nodded. 'Yes,' he said.

'In that case you'd better come in and close the door.'

Trev looked at us and then did as he was told.

'What's your name?'

'Trev,' said Trev. Then he coughed and corrected himself. 'Trevor.'

'Have you got another name?'

'Yes.'

We all looked at Trev with interest. He'd never told us he had another name.

'Well, what is it?' the woman asked. I could tell she was getting irritable.

Trev looked at the floor and mumbled something.

'What?' said the woman.

'Gerard,' said Trev.

Fancy Trev being called Gerard. I looked at him and nearly laughed out loud.

Trev clenched his fist at his side and gave it a slight shake. He narrowed his eyes at me.

'No,' said the woman looking at the ceiling in exasperation. 'Your surname.'

'Oh, er . . .' he frowned for a second. 'Morpeth,' he said.

'Mmh,' said the woman. She picked up the blue diary and leafed through it. 'Nobody sees Mr Braithwaite without an appointment, you know. I suggest you write a letter explaining your reasons for wanting to see him. And if Mr Braithwaite wants to see you we'll write suggesting a day and the time.'

'But we did,' said Frankie. 'We did make an appointment.'

I thought she'd gone mad.

'We wrote to you.'

'You wrote?'

'Oh yes.' Frankie gave a little laugh, 'Should I have brought the letter? I'm sorry, I left it at home.'

What was she talking about? Trev looked at Frankie his eyes wide. Then he looked at me. Then at the woman then back at Frankie again. He thought she'd gone mad, too.

The woman raised her eyebrows. 'I see, and what would the name be?'

'Diane,' said Frankie, without hesitation.

'I beg your pardon?' said the woman.

'Diane,' said Frankie again, smiling sweetly. 'Diane Anderson.'

The woman looked hard at Frankie. And Frankie looked straight back.

I was out of my depth. I sneaked a look at Trev. His eyes looked as though they might end up on the carpet any minute. I shook my head. I had no idea what was going on either.

The woman looked down at the book. 'Diane Anderson?'

'Diane R. Anderson,' said Frankie.

The woman's head came slowly up from the

diary and she gazed steadily at Frankie. I had the feeling she didn't believe her but there wasn't much she could do about it.

'Diane R. Anderson,' she said.

'That's right,' said Frankie. I don't know how she managed to keep a straight face.

'I see,' said the woman. 'Your appointment's for half past eleven, you know.'

'I know. I came early. I hope that's all right.'

The girl closed the diary with a snap.

She pressed a button on the intercom.

'There's a Diane R. Anderson to see you, Mr Braithwaite. I'm afraid she's rather early. Do you want to see her now?'

She nodded her head as Mr Braithwaite spoke then she looked up at Frankie.

'Mr Braithwaite will see you now.'

She managed to make her voice sound surprised. She held open the door for us. We walked into the office. First Frankie, then me and Sam, then Trev.

Mr Braithwaite was standing with his back to us looking at a map on the wall. The door closed behind us. We stood there, shuffling. He turned his head and stared at Frankie for a couple of seconds, smiled, then turned and wrote something on the map. We looked at one another. I wished I was at home having my dinner. I crossed my legs. Being nervous made me want to go to the toilet even more.

'You wanted to see me, Miss Anderson?' he said, without looking round.

It took Frankie by surprise.

Mr Braithwaite spun round. 'Miss Anderson?' he said in a questioning voice. 'I suppose that must be you?'

Frankie nodded. 'Yes,' she said.

'Mmh,' the man murmured. He smiled. 'Well, it is nice to see you.' He smiled. 'Prompt too.'

We weren't sure if we were supposed to say anything. Mr Braithwaite didn't give us a chance. He gave me the feeling that he knew all about us.

He leaned with both hands on the window sill.

'It's a wonderful view up here, isn't it?'

He looked at us. He was still smiling. His hair was stiff and stuck out at the back. He smoothed it with the flat of his hand.

'But, of course, I don't suppose you've ever been up here before. Why don't you have a look?'

We hesitated.

'Go on. Don't be afraid. I won't bite you.'

We went over and looked down on the town. I could see Grace Park and the canal on the far left hand side, the cars on Scarisbrick New Road and the towers of the Cottage Hospital.

'Heh, there's our house,' said Sam.

I couldn't help wishing I was back there.

Mr Braithwaite said, 'Fascinating, isn't it? Gives you a whole new perspective. You can probably see your school, do you see over there to the west?'

We all looked in the direction he was pointing.

'Of course, I'm very friendly with Mr Liversedge. Very friendly indeed. You know Mr Liversedge, of course.'

'He's our Headmaster, sir,' said Trev.

'Yes, we're very good friends, very good friends indeed. If I get to know that any pupils have been misbehaving I know I only have to get on the phone to Mr Liversedge and the matter will be dealt with.'

I remember seeing a film once of a snake and a rabbit. The rabbit just sat there shaking, staring at the snake. That's how it felt being with Mr Braithwaite. And we were the rabbits.

Then Mr Braithwaite did something very clever. Very suddenly he said, 'Well, Diane?'

Frankie was caught by surprise. She didn't look round.

Then she remembered. But she turned too late.

We all looked at Mr Braithwaite. Frankie started to speak but before she could say anything the door was opened by the secretary.

'Yes?' said Mr Braithwatie.

'Miss Anderson to see you,' said the secretary.

A tall middle-aged woman walked in.

'Good afternoon, Diane,' said Mr Braithwaite, 'how nice to see you.'

Mr Braithwaite looked at us. We looked at the floor.

The lady said, 'Oh Adrian, I'm sorry, I didn't know you were busy.'

Sam was hiding behind me.

Mr Braithwaite said, 'It's all right, Diane.

Perhaps you can help me with a bit of a problem.'

He looked at us. I shuffled.

'Rather a strange coincidence. One of those curious things that happens once in a lifetime, really. I wonder if it's ever happened to you?'

'What's that?' said the lady called Diane.

'Well, two people with exactly the same name. Even down to the initial. And would you believe both have an appointment at precisely the same time.'

'Oh, what name is that?'

'Diane Anderson.'

'You mean my name?' She looked at Frankie. 'And you mean this girl's name . . .'

'Yes. Diane Anderson, too.' He walked over to the window and looked out.

'Isn't that so?'

'No,' said Frankie.

'No? But I'm sure you said your name was Diane Anderson, too. That was the name you gave my secretary. Or perhaps she misheard. Well?'

He came in front of Frankie and stared at her. Frankie didn't say anything.

'What is your name, then?'

Frankie bit her lip. 'Frankie,' she said.

'Frankie,' Mr Braithwaite said. He looked at the ceiling. 'Mmh, unusual name for a girl. What's your real name?'

'Francesca.'

'And the surname?'

'DeLange.'

'Francesca DeLange.'

'Yes.'

'Ah. But you told me your name was Diane Anderson. Now why was that?'

'I don't know.'

'Don't know? But you did call yourself Diane Anderson. Are you in the habit of taking other people's names?'

'No.'

'It can get you into a lot of trouble you know. Legally it's called false pretences. I've known people go to prison for doing it.' He smiled. 'But you promise me that you've never done it before?'

'No,' said Frankie.

'Mmh.'

The door opened. The woman we'd passed on the stairs came in.

'Yes, Angela,' said Mr Braithwaite. The secretary stood behind her in the doorway. Suddenly the room was full of people.

The lady said, 'I'm sorry, Mr Braithwaite.'

'No, come on in, Angela, you might as well. Everybody else seems to be in the room.'

She began to speak and then saw Frankie.

'Ah, so Celia found you.'

Mr Braithwaite looked at her. He shook his head.

'Celia?' he said in bewilderment.

'Yes, Celia. Your daughter.'

'What about her?'

'She's there.'

Mr Braithwaite looked round.

'Where?' he said.

Angela pointed at Frankie. 'There,' she said.

Mr Braithwaite pinched the bridge of his nose and closed both his eyes. He sighed.

'This is proving to be a very difficult morning.'

Frankie said, 'I can explain.'

'I'm sure you can.'

'Look.' He turned to the three women. 'I wonder if you could leave me alone with this young lady for a moment, please.'

The women looked at him.

'Please,' he repeated.

He turned to Trev, Sam and me. 'Would you mind waiting outside as well? I want to talk to this young lady alone.'

Somebody said in a loud voice, 'No, we have to stay together.'

I looked round to see who had spoken and realized it was me.

'Very well,' said Mr Braithwaite.

The three ladies left the room.

Mr Braithwaite sat down and took off his spectacles and smoothed down his hair again.

'Now, what's all this about? First you say you're Diane, then I learn you've been impersonating my daughter. Do you have any more rôles?'

Frankie drew a deep breath. 'We didn't want to do it. I've never done it before. It's just that we had to see you. And nobody would let us in. If they'd let us in I wouldn't have had to pretend to be someone else. I only did that because we'd

126

been wronged in the first place and it's no good saying two wrongs don't make a right because I know that's true but if we hadn't done that wrong we wouldn't have been here at all and you would never have known about it.'

Frankie stopped. It had been a long speech. We all stared at Mr Braithwaite.

'I don't understand a word of what you're saying. Would you start at the beginning, please.'

I didn't think it was fair that Frankie should take all the blame. I thought the more we stuck together the better it would be.

I blurted out before Frankie could say any more.

'It started with Grace Park.'

'Grace . . .?' said Mr Braithwaite. 'Is she someone else you've been impersonating?'

'It's not a person. It's a place. Grace Park.'

Mr Braithwaite struck his forehead as if he'd just got the answer to a problem. 'Ah, that Grace Park!'

Then I told him how I'd found the fence that night and how we'd been playing there for years and how we'd gone down to play the 22nd replay of the Final but we hadn't been able to get in and how the doorman hadn't given him our letter. It all just came pouring out. When I'd finished there was a silence. Then Mr Braithwaite said,

'Well, I can sympathize with what you're saying but you know you have to follow the rules in this life. Suppose everybody burst in unannounced as you did? It wouldn't be fair on all the others, would it?' He pointed at the map on the wall. 'You see, this is the plan for Grace Park. It is going to cost fifteen million pounds. There'll be supermarkets, an indoor arena, parking for two thousand cars, restaurants, theatres and on top of that it's going to give a lot of work to a great number of people. You wouldn't want to take that work away from them, would you? No, of course you wouldn't. So you see, we're not taking your playing field away from you without thinking very seriously about it. And we haven't forgotten about you, either. Don't get that idea into your heads. We think very highly of our young people in this town and I wouldn't want to be Town Clerk if that wasn't true. You're very important to us and I want you to remember that. And we want you to have lots of healthy exercise, so in the plan we've provided places to play. Special purpose-built play centres for you kids. Don't you think that will be nice?'

Frankie said, 'But it won't be Grace Park. It's ours. Nobody ever went there. And now everybody will be there. It was ours.'

All four of us murmured in assent.

'It'll all be hidden,' I said. 'Where Grandad took the penalty.'

'Grandad?' Mr Braithwaite looked bewildered.

My mouth started talking again without me knowing where it was going. It all came tumbling out in one breath.

'He scored a penalty. He could have gone to Arsenal. But he stayed even though thingummy the director man came in his big car and gave him dinner but Grandad didn't want to have dinner he wanted to play in the Final he said and they had a penalty so he scored and then he scored against Arsenal and they were in the Final but his leg was broken through his sock and he never played again ever and no one will ever know because it'll all be concrete and shops but if it wasn't people would be able to see, wouldn't they?'

They all looked at me. I could see they had as much idea what I was talking about as Mr Braithwaite.

He said, 'Look, I know you feel very strongly about this. And I admire your courage, your initiative, in coming up here. I really do. I think you kids have been absolutely super. But there are two sides to every question. What I want you to do now is to leave me to think about it. Will you do that? And I promise you I'll give it my most serious consideration.'

He leaned towards us.

'Now, you're sensible kids. I can see that. I want you to do something for me, will you do that?'

'Yes,' said Sam.

Mr Braithwaite nodded seriously at Sam as though he'd said something very wise.

'I know you will, and that's why I feel I can say this to you. There's not many kids I'd say this to. What I want you to do is to trust me. Will you do that? Will you?'

He looked at each of us in turn. Frankie

didn't say anything. The three of us said 'Yes.'

Mr Braithwaite looked at Frankie.

'Well?' he said.

Frankie began. 'The letter . . .'

But Mr Braithwaite took the letter gently from her.

'Leave the letter with me. Will you do that? Now I promise you I'll read it very carefully. And what I'll do is this; I'll give it my most serious consideration. Now I can't say fairer than that, can I?'

He looked round at us and smiled, then he pushed a button on the intercom on his desk.

'Eileen, ask Blenkinsopp to come up.' He came over and stood in front of us, smiling.

'Now, I want to shake your hands before you go. Just to show we understand each other and there are no hard feelings.'

He shook each of our hands in turn. When he shook mine he squeezed really hard, but I wasn't going to show him it hurt.

'Now, what are your names?'

Before I could stop him Trev said, 'They're all on the letter.'

I wished that we hadn't put our names on.

'Of course. On the letter,' said Mr Braithwaite. He smiled.

The intercom crackled. The secretary's voice said, 'Mr Blenkinsopp's here, Mr Braithwaite.'

Mr Braithwaite spoke into the intercom. 'Fine, show him in, Eileen.' As he spoke he smiled and winked at us.

The door opened and the doorman came in.

When he saw us I thought he was going to explode.

Mr Braithwaite said, 'Ah, Mr Blenkinsopp, escort these young friends of mine to the door, would you?'

Mr Blenkinsopp held open the door. He still looked as if he was going to explode. We filed past him, trying not to grin or laugh. He closed the door behind us and then we were in the corridor. He marched in front of us, swinging his arms. We marched along behind him. Trev began to march like him. He marched really close behind him swinging his arms in a daft way. We all joined on behind. It was like an army march past. We got to the lift. I suddenly remembered how I wanted to go to the toilet. I said to Mr Blenkinsopp,

'Excuse me, I have to go to the toilet.'

Mr Blenkinsopp said, 'It's back the way you came. We'll wait for you downstairs.'

I ran back down the corridor past the office we'd just been in. There was a silhouette on the door. I knew that meant 'gents'. Inside, a bald headed man was bending over the wash basin with his back towards me washing his hands. It was Mr Braithwaite. On the wash basin beside him was a black hairy object. He stroked his bald head with both hands then picked up the hairy object and fixed it carefully on his head. Gently he smoothed it into place. He hadn't seen me. I closed the door quietly and then ran down the corridor and raced down the stairs after the others.

10

Back at school after the summer holidays I was put in 3D, Mr Daniel's class. 3D was a lower class than I'd been in before. You weren't supposed to know that; that's why all the classes were called after the teacher's initials. But everybody did. Mr Daniel had short black hair and a moustache and took Games and PE. He always wore a tracksuit and trainers and had a whistle round his neck. After calling the register he made a speech about how important it was to make a fresh start and how he wanted us to be a credit to 3D. He said he'd play fair by us if we played fair by him. All sorts of rubbish like that. Then we had a long assembly that went on until break where we sang this hymn about how glad we were to be back at school and Mr Liversedge made a speech about God and litter. I looked round for Frankie but I couldn't see her. Then I remembered she'd been given extra holiday until half term so that she could be with her dad in Belgium. He'd wanted them to get to know one another again. She thought he was going to tell her that he and her mum were going to get back together again. She never talked about it much but I knew that's what she was hoping.

After break, Mr Daniel said he had to go and sort out the PE kit and we could either write about what we wanted to be when we grew up or about what we'd done in our summer holidays. I didn't want to write about either. The only thing being in 3D qualified you for was being a layabout. And we hadn't done anything in the summer holidays. I'd gone with Dad, Sam and Andrew to stay at my Auntie Maud's in Morecambe for a week but that had been boring. Trev and me had tried to cycle to Southport one day but he'd got a puncture in his back tyre before we'd even got past the Co-op in Scarisbrick New Road and we'd had to walk home again. With Frankie being away it had been one of the most boring summer holidays I'd ever had. I looked at my exercise book and wrote the date. I couldn't think of anything. My mind was a blank. In the end I wrote a lot of rubbish about how brilliant a footballer I was and how one day I'd play for England. Lies like that.

For the last lesson we had this student for Environmental Studies. You could always tell when it was a student because they were always dead young and never told you off and you were always doing projects. This student was called Miss Slaney and she wore her hair in a tail at the back tied up in a red scarf. As soon as she walked in the class carrying this big holdall stuffed with papers, Andy Wall started giving low whistles and goggling his eyes. She went a bit pink round the throat but pretended she hadn't heard.

'Right, 3D,' she said, 'every Monday during this period we're going to be working on an exciting new project called Transport.'

Everybody groaned. We'd done transport with the last student in Mrs Bell's class. Miss Slaney's mouth twitched and she pulled at her hair. She tried to smile.

'I thought you'd all find that interesting,' she said. 'Now, I wonder who can tell me what transport means?'

Nobody got a chance to answer because a kid from the first year came round with a message from Mr Backhouse about the school play he was doing at the end of term.

Miss Slaney said, '*Oliver Twist* is a jolly exciting play and I'm sure lots of people will want to be in it. Don't forget, a meeting in the main hall at dinner time. Here's your chance to be stars, 3D.' And she laughed, trying to get us on her side, but nobody else joined in.

'Right,' she went on, 'we were talking about transport.' She knelt down and took a huge sheaf of maps and walls charts and graphs out of a basket. 'Who can tell me what form of transport they used to come to school this morning?'

What I can never understand about teachers is why they keep asking you questions about things you know nothing about. If they know all about it, why don't they just tell us instead of wasting time?

I was sitting next to Andy Wall. I thought he might start talking about the fight we'd had on the sandhills when we'd been in the Juniors. But he seemed to have forgotten all about it. He put his hand up right away. He was brilliant at wasting time. He had this trick of repeating the last word that teachers said, pretending he couldn't understand. It wouldn't have worked with Mr Daniel, he'd have spotted right away that Andy was trying to take the mick but with a student it could hardly fail.

Miss Slaney brightened up when she saw Andy's hand was up.

'Yes, er . . .' she tried to remember Andy's name. 'Yes, Hall,' she said brightly, 'you had your hand up.'

'Wall,' said Andy.

'Wall?' said Miss Slaney. 'Well, no, I don't think you'd call a wall a means of transport. Although you could walk on it. Perhaps that's what you were thinking.'

'Wall not Hall, Miss.'

'Wall?'

'It's my name, Miss.'

'Name?'

'Yes, Miss. You called me Hall but my name's Wall.'

'Oh, I'm sorry,' said Miss Slaney, 'I thought you had your hand up.'

I could see Andy was getting into gear. With any luck he'd be able to keep this going until dinner time.

'Hand?' he said as if he'd never heard the word before.

'Yes, hand,' said Miss Slaney, 'you had it in the air.'

'Air?' said Andy looking up.

Miss Slaney sighed, 'Yes, you had your hand in the air when you asked the question.'

Andy frowned and looked puzzled. 'Question?'

Miss Slaney closed her eyes in exasperation. 'Yes, I asked you about transport. What it was and how you came to school. Why did you put your hand up?'

'Hand?' said Andy. He looked at his hand as if the answer might be written on it.

'You put it up.'

'We have to put it up, Miss.'

'Yes, but why?'

'It's a rule, Miss. If we want to answer a question we have to put our hands up.'

Miss Slaney breathed out heavily. She looked tired already. 'I see, well, what was your answer?'

'It wasn't an answer, Miss, I just wanted to say about transport, Miss.'

'What did you want to say?'

'We done it last year, Miss.'

'Last year?'

Miss Slaney looked sad and disappointed.

'Yeah, with Mrs Bell, Miss.' He turned round to the rest of the class. 'Didn't we do it last year?'

Everybody started shouting out at once, giving bits of information.

Miss Slaney clapped her hands. 'That'll do, 3D. Settle down now or I'll . . .'

We never found out what she might have

136

done because another messenger knocked on the door. Miss Slaney raised her eyebrows. It would be dinner time in ten minutes. She could see she was never going to get to the end of this lesson.

'What is it now?' she said, putting her hand to her forehead.

'Please, Miss, Mr Liversedge says Benbow has to go to his office now, Miss.'

I went cold when I heard my name.

Andy Wall said, 'Yah, Benbow, you're for it.'

I couldn't think what I'd done.

'Benbow? Is he here?' asked Miss Slaney.

I stood up.

'You'd better go along,' she said.

I walked slowly to the door and opened it. As I closed it behind me I heard Miss Slaney saying, 'Now, who can tell me what form of transport involves your feet?'

Walking across the hall I was thinking I'd rather be with Miss Slaney doing boring old transport than going to see Mr Liversedge. I'd rather be jumping out of a plane without a parachute than going to see Mr Liversedge. I kept turning over in my mind the things I might have done wrong. But it was only the first day. I'd have had to have been a master criminal to have done anything seriously wrong in that time.

I turned the corner and there, sitting on a chair outside Mr Liversedge's office, was Trev. He was biting his nails and staring anxiously at the floor. He looked up as I sat next to him.

'He wants you as well, then?'

I nodded. 'What d'you think he wants us for?'

Trev shrugged. 'Search me,' he said.

The door opened and Mr Liversedge came out, looking stern. He frowned when he saw us. 'Benbow, Trevor. Inside!' he said.

We walked past him and into his office.

11

Mr Liversedge sat down at his desk. We both stood looking at the floor. Outside I could hear the lawn mower moving backwards and forwards across the playing fields. He wrote something in a book, then threw the pen down and looked at us over the top of his glasses. One of his eyelids drooped lower than the other.

'I suppose you know what this is all about, don't you?' he said.

Teachers are always saying things like that. I hadn't the foggiest idea what I was supposed to have done. I tried to think, but there was nothing. Nothing at all. One minute I'd been sitting in my class listening to Miss Slaney telling us all about transport and the next I was in Mr Liversedge's office. It was a mystery. I looked at Trev but he was looking out of the window. I noticed we both had our hands behind our backs and were standing in exactly the same position. I didn't want anybody to think I was copying Trev. I hate copying anybody. I held my hands in front of me and brought my feet together.

Mr Liversedge said, 'For heaven's sake, stop shuffling and stand still.'

He came out from behind his desk and stood

looking at both of us. I tried to keep looking him straight in the eye like Frankie would have done but he was too near. He was so close I could see all the pores on his skin and the little ginger hairs curling out of his nostrils.

'I'm waiting for an answer, Benbow.'

'I don't know, sir.'

Mr Liversedge shook his head.

'Don't know. Don't know. That's always the easy answer, isn't it, Benbow, don't know?'

'But I don't, honest, sir.'

'Don't you answer me back,' said Mr Liversedge.

I thought you could never win with teachers. First they told you off for not answering and then when you answered you got told off for saying something.

'You've been a rebel ever since you came to this school, haven't you, Benbow? The moment you walked through those school gates you decided you were going to make life as difficult as possible for all of us. You had some brains somewhere but you're just too lazy to use them. And where are you now? In 3D. What d'you think your mother and father are going to think when they hear about that, eh? And it's a shame really because *you* know and *I* know that you're capable of doing far better. But you've got this self-destructive streak in you. Lord knows where it comes from. Now, you can spoil your own life if you want to, Benbow, that's your prerogative, but when you start dragging other people down with you, well, that's when I'm going to come down on you and come down hard. I know you put up Francesca there to wanting to play football for the school team and then doing everything you could to draw attention to yourself. And then there was that other business with the food. Where you learned those disgusting habits, I don't know.'

I could feel Mr Liversedge's breath banging against my face as he spoke; could see the fillings in his teeth, smell his breath. What was he going on at me like this for? There were worse kids than me. The idea that I could lead Frankie on was stupid. She was the one who had done the leading. Mr Liversedge went quiet, just staring at me and breathing hard. I tried to keep looking at him but he was so close it was making my eyes cross over. The bell for dinner time rang loudly. He drew himself back, folded his arms and stared at the ceiling before walking round the back of us. I couldn't hear his footsteps on the carpet. I got the feeling he might clout me from behind any minute. I tried not to flinch. I looked round the room trying to take my mind off what was happening. There was a picture of the girls' netball team on one wall and next to it a wooden cross. Beyond that was the panelled wall of his office. The top half was made of glass. On it was a picture of Jesus holding a lantern, knocking on a door in a forest. It looked out on to the hall but you couldn't see out because the glass was all different colours. There was a small hole in the glass just underneath the lantern. Every now and then you'd see somebody's head walking past. I wondered if Mr Liversedge had made the hole on purpose so he could see what was going on in the hall. I recognized Mr Backhouse walking past it for a second giving books out. Then he became blurred again. A group of kids were sitting down on a bench. I suppose they were there to audition for the school play.

Mr Liversedge had started on Trev now.

'And I suppose you don't know what I'm talking about, either?'

Trev just shrugged his shoulders. He moved his knee backwards and forwards nervously.

I kept my eyes on the hole. It was like watching a film. A girl with long red hair came and sat down on the bench. She was talking to somebody. Every now and then her head moved outside the frame of the hole and became blurred and shadowy. Then it came back again. She stood up for a moment and I could see she was wearing a green skirt. She looked familiar. Then I saw it was Frankie. But it couldn't be her. She was staying with her dad in Belgium. She wouldn't be back until after half term. Anyway, Frankie had short hair and always wore jeans. It was like looking at a stranger. It was funny watching her when she didn't know I could see her. She pushed her fingers through her hair then laughed at something somebody said. I had this strange feeling coming over me just from looking at her. It was like a wave passing slowly down my body. Like an aching feeling that I'd never had before. That I couldn't put a name to. For a minute I thought I was going to faint. Then she looked straight at me in a way that made me feel that she could see me; knew what I was feeling. I tried to pull my eyes away but I didn't seem able to. My face was burning. I could feel it turning red. I wondered if Mr Liversedge would notice. I had a feeling he would be able to tell what I was thinking just by looking at me.

'Don't you care about anybody?'

For a second I didn't know where I was. I didn't know who I was. I shook my head. It was like being in a dream.

'Do you? Do you care about anybody or anything apart from yourself? Are you listening to me?' Mr Liversedge shouted.

'Sir?' I said.

'You haven't taken in one word I've said have you, Benbow? Not one word.'

He walked across in front of me blocking my vision. I couldn't see her any more. I couldn't see her. How could she be there and in Belgium at the same time? Perhaps I'd imagined it. I wanted to push him out of the way. He shook his head at me and walked over to the window. I looked through the missing pane, but she was gone. Alan Maitland was there, combing his hair.

'HAVE YOU?'

'Yes, sir, I have,' I said automatically.

'You say you have but I know you, Benbow. You nod your head, you say – Yes sir, No sir. But I know you haven't taken a blind bit of notice. NOT ONE BIT.'

He had this habit of speaking very, very quietly and then shouting the last word so that it made you jump out of your skin. It made you deaf for about five minutes after.

'Sir, what am I supposed to . . .'

I didn't get a chance.

'Don't you answer me back, Benbow.'

'Sir, I . . .'

'BE QUIET!'

In the silence I could feel my ears ringing. 'You haven't got the courage to do things yourself so what you do is you get others to do things for you. First that girl, then Morpeth here, but worst of all, most despicable of you, your little brother. Do you know I had to phone Mrs Woodhead at the Junior School and tell her what you'd led your little brother into? Don't you have any sense of responsibility to your younger brother? He probably looks up to you, God help us. I know your type, Benbow. Don't think I don't. I'm just about fed up with your attitude.'

I still couldn't work out what he was getting at.

'This may be something you don't understand, Benbow, but I'm proud of this school; proud of its achievements, proud of what it stands for. And then something like this happens.'

He waved a letter in the air and stuck it under both our noses.

'I presume you recognize this letter.'

It was the letter we'd left with Mr Braithwaite, and there at the bottom were all our names. Suddenly I realized what all the fuss was about. Mr

Braithwaite had asked us to trust him and we'd believed him.

'Well? Do you recognize it?'

'Yes, sir,' we both mumbled.

'And what have you got to say?'

There was nothing we could say.

'What ever d'you think you're up to? Bursting in on the Town Clerk like that. Telling lies. Wasting his time. Have you any idea how busy a man he is? Have you? D'you think he's got nothing more important to do than deal with trivialities such as THIS?'

He ended up on one of his shouts. I was thinking how I never knew what was important until somebody told me about it. I didn't think what we'd done was so bad. I could imagine if it had been in a history book we'd have probably got medals for it. But now Mr Liversedge was making such a big thing of it I realized it must be bad. It must be bad otherwise he wouldn't have made such a fuss. Maybe it was trivial, after all. Who cared if we never played on Grace Park, anyway? Only us. And John Stokes probably wasn't going to play again. And Trev had told me that Carlton's mum wouldn't let him speak to us any more. She thought we were a bad influence. And Frankie had said she was losing interest. There was only Sam, Trev and me left. I had this feeling that we wouldn't play any more of those Finals, anywhere. It wasn't really worth getting into trouble about.

'Well, what are you going to do about it?'

I shrugged. 'I don't know, sir.'

'Don't know? Well, I know. I know what you're going to do about it.'

He sat down behind his desk. 'And that's not the end of it. Not by a long chalk. I've had a phone call from Carlton Griffiths's mother about all the trouble you've been getting him into. Holding up the traffic in the middle of town. Did you ever stop to think what kind of impression that gave of this school? Did you? No, of course not, that would be asking too much. You'd have to be considering somebody else's feelings besides your own, wouldn't you, and that would be asking too much in your case.'

He walked towards the big cupboards against the windows. I thought, that's where the cane must be. I wondered if he would cane Trev? Perhaps he'd cane me twice as much. Once for me and once for getting Sam, Frankie, Trev and John Stokes into trouble. Andy Wall had once had the cane off him for setting the toilets on fire. He told me Mr Liversedge had smashed his arm playing rugby and had to cane you back handed. He even had to do a little run up. He opened a drawer and took out a piece of paper. Then he said quietly, 'I want you to write a letter of apology to Mr Braithwaite, saying how sorry you are for wasting his time. Saying you'll never do such a thing again. I want this letter written and posted before Friday.'

'But sir . . .'

'FRIDAY! Do you understand? Or if you

prefer I can think of a worse punishment.' He nodded his head in the direction of the cupboard. 'Do you understand what I'm talking about?'

I understood all right. I took the paper from him.

He went back to the cupboard to get an envelope.

Mr Liversedge handed me the envelope.

'I'm going to trust you to post it, Benbow. But just remember this, I'll be talking to Mr Braithwaite. Mr Braithwaite happens to be a very good friend of mine. So I shall know, mark my words, I shall know.'

'Yes sir.'

He looked at us both for a few seconds and then said quietly, 'You may go.'

We opened the door and walked out into the hall.

'Phew,' Trev said.

It was like when you come out of the swimming pool after doing a length under water or when you go out into the street for the first time after being ill in bed.

We walked past this group of kids who were sitting round Mr Backhouse. He was saying, 'So, remember, auditions in the drama studio on Tuesday and Thursday. Lots of parts and, remember, experience isn't necessary, what we want is bags of enthusiasm. Any questions?'

We tiptoed past. I didn't want to get involved in any plays. I looked at the place where I thought I'd seen Frankie. Alan Maitland was sitting on a bench leafing through a copy of *Oliver Twist*. I stopped near him and looked round. I must have been dreaming. Or perhaps I'd seen a ghost. Marion Archard was sitting next to Alan Maitland. Perhaps it had been her I'd seen. Her hair was a reddish colour.

Alan Maitland said, 'Have you come for an audition or are you waiting for a bus?'

'Come on,' said Trev.

Marion Archard said, 'Are you g-g-going to read for the p-p-play?'

I shook my head. I wondered how she was going to get a part with a stutter like that.

'No more questions?' said Mr Backhouse. 'See you all on Tuesday or Thursday then.' He pointed at me. 'How about you, Benbow? Are we going to have the pleasure of your company at the auditions?'

'No fear, sir,' I called and everybody laughed.

We walked out into the playground. Some first-years were rushing around kicking a tennis ball.

'Coming for a kick around?' asked Trev.

'Shut up,' I said.

'What's up with you then?'

'Nothing,' I said, 'nothing's up with me.'

I walked over to the wall and leaned on it. Trev was haring round the playground running rings round all these first-years. I screwed the envelope and paper into a ball and threw it onto the ground. The wind picked it up and blew it across the wall and down the street until I couldn't see it any more.

12

That night Dr Naysmith came to see Grandad while Mum and Dad were out. Grandad was sitting in a cane chair in the greenhouse covered in tartan blankets, watching the old black and white telly that we kept in there. The picture made it look as if there was a blizzard and he had the sound turned up full volume. All round me the panes of glass rattled in their frames. I thought the whole greenhouse was going to collapse round our ears any minute. There was one of those awards programmes on the telly where famous film stars in fancy clothes run on to a stage looking surprised and say how grateful they are and that they don't really deserve the award because they couldn't have won it without loads of other people. Grandad was only watching because he thought Mum might be on it. Even though he disapproved of her being an actress he watched anything about actors in the hope of seeing her. He would never admit it, but secretly he was proud of her. Every time there was a picture of the audience he kept shouting out, 'There she is, that's her! Did you see her? Did you see your mum?'

'She's not there at all, Grandad.'

'I saw her. In a black frock with a shiny hat.'

It wasn't even a woman. It was a fat man wearing a dinner jacket.

'It's not a shiny hat, Grandad. It's a man with a bald head.'

All this time the sound was pouring round us like a tidal wave.

'You what?'

'IT'S A MAN. WITH A BALD HEAD.'

'Of course she hasn't.'

'NO, NOT MUM, THE MAN, THE MAN HAS A BALD HEAD.'

But by the time I'd made myself heard over the racket, he'd seen her somewhere else. He saw Mum everywhere. Once he even thought she was a statue.

'She's not there at all Grandad. She's doing a commercial about sausages.'

'You what?'

'SAUSAGES.'

'No thanks,' he said and pulled the blanket round his chin and started grumbling to himself. 'Should never have bought her that piano. That was the beginning of it.'

It got a bit interesting when this Australian actor instead of saying 'thank you' like everybody else had done, made a speech about how the white man had driven the aborigines out of their home-lands and that Australia belonged to them really and should be given back. People started booing and shouting and a fight started at the back of the hall. The actor said he was accepting the award on behalf of the aborigines and he held it high in the air and waved it about. Two men tried to drag him off the stage but he just carried on shouting. A lady in a long black dress who was giving out the awards was knocked on to the floor and you could see all her legs. There was pandemonium. I really enjoyed it.

Grandad pointed at the mass of bodies scrimmaging at the front. 'There she is,' he shouted joyfully. 'There she is!'

The front door bell rang and I showed Dr Naysmith in. Dr Naysmith had a round, shiny face and was always rubbing his hands together and smiling as if everything was exciting and interesting.

He opened Grandad's pyjama top and put the stethoscope against his chest. Then he made him bend forward and did the same for his back.

'Fuss about nothing,' Grandad grumbled to himself.

'Ah ha. Ah ha!' said Dr Naysmith as if Grandad's chest was the most exciting thing in the world. 'Had a bit of a funny turn, did we?'

'That was last night. I'm fine now. Don't know what they're making all the fuss about.'

The doctor wound a black bandage round Grandad's arm and squeezed a black bulb rapidly.

'Water works all right?'

' 'Course they are,' said Grandad. 'Mind your own business.'

'You are my business,' said Dr Naysmith chuckling. He glanced up at the television.

'Likes watching films, does he?'

'He thinks my mum's there,' I said.

'What you whispering for?' said Grandad.

'We were saying your daughter's there. YOUR DAUGHTER.'

' 'Course she's not. Don't be daft. She's doing an advert for sausages,' said Grandad.

Somebody tapped on the greenhouse window. I shaded my eyes and looked out. A girl with long hair was standing there with her back to me. She turned and looked at me. It was Frankie.

'You go on,' said Dr Naysmith. 'I can let myself out.'

I went out into the back garden. Frankie was leaning on next door's wall with her back to me.

I said, 'I thought you were staying at your dad's till half term.'

She didn't turn and look at me.

'I was.'

'Why have you come back early?'

'Reasons,' she said.

She didn't seem to want to talk. I wanted to tell her about how I thought I'd seen her through Liversedge's window. That I thought she'd been a ghost. She'd laugh at that. It was getting dark. I put my hands in my pockets and leaned against the greenhouse. There was a sharp, sweet smell in the air. I realized Frankie must have been wearing perfume. Just for something to say I said, 'Grandad's got the doctor in.'

She didn't even look at me.

'He fell down in the hall yesterday. It was a

heart attack but the doctor said it wasn't serious.'

It was as though she hadn't heard. She started walking up and down the path slowly, looking at the ground. I wondered what was up with her. Usually she couldn't stop talking. She hunched her shoulders and bit her lip. I wondered why she'd come over. It was as though she knew what I was thinking.

'I have to get some papers from the car. Mum wants to sell it.'

Since her dad had gone to Belgium they kept their car in our garage. Mum kept her rusty old Mini in the front.

'Why?'

'Because she wants some money. Why else would anybody sell a car?'

'I thought it was your dad's car.'

She walked away from me and didn't answer. It was like talking to a stranger. She looked different, too, with her hair long. She took the car key out of the pocket of her frock. I thought I'd try and make her laugh.

'Hey, Mr Liversedge had me and Trev in this morning. You know, that man we went to see at the Town Hall, Mr Braithwaite, well, he rang up Mr Liversedge and told him everything. I thought he was going to cane us. But he said we've to write a letter and apologize. He said it was all my fault. That I led you on. Imagine me doing that, Frankie.'

She just looked at me with no expression on her face.

I thought I'd tell her about how I'd seen her through the glass that morning. How I'd nearly passed out.

'You know that stained glass picture of Jesus in Liversedge's office . . .' I stopped. It didn't seem the right time to tell her about it. I wanted to tell her lots of things but it didn't feel natural somehow.

'What were you going to say?'

'Nothing,' I said, 'it was nothing.'

She shivered. 'It's cold out here,' she said. 'Let's go in the garage.'

I opened the garage door and switched on the light but it wasn't working. The car almost filled the garage. There was no room to sit.

She turned the key in the door.

'Let's sit inside,' she said.

We squeezed in and I sat in the driver's seat. It smelled of petrol and plastic. I ran my hands over the steering wheel. Frankie was staring straight ahead. I turned on the interior switch but nothing happened. I guessed the battery must have been flat. When Frankie had first stayed at our house we'd often sat in the car and gone on imaginary journeys. All over the world, we'd gone.

'It'd be great to just start the engine and drive off into the night. Just go anywhere and never come back,' I said. 'Remember how we used to do that?'

'We were kids then,' she said. 'You do stupid things when you're kids.'

It didn't sound like Frankie talking. There was

154

a long silence. I could hear the freezer humming and the sound of our television. I wondered if they were still fighting and rolling about. I thought of telling her about the television programme but I couldn't bring the words out. I turned to look at her and gave a cough. But she didn't turn round. It was as if she was on her own. For the first time in my life I started to feel embarrassed being with her. It was the silence. I thought, I won't say anything. If she doesn't want to say anything that's fine. I'm not going to be the first one to speak. It was always me that did that. For once I'll just keep my mouth shut. See how she likes it! The silence seemed to go on and on. I shifted in my seat. It creaked softly.

I said, 'When Liversedge said about it all being my fault, I didn't let on about it being your idea. I don't think he'll want to see you.'

That wasn't what had actually happened, but Mr Liversedge *had* blamed me for everything so it came to the same thing. I looked at her. She was still staring straight out of the windscreen. It was as though she was looking down a long road. That she could see for miles and miles.

'D'you think we ought to send that letter?' I asked her.

She sniffed and wiped her nose with a tissue.

'Letter?' she said.

'The letter Old Liversedge said we should write, d'you think we ought to send it?'

'How should I know?' she snapped. 'What's the point of *not* sending it? That battle's over. Have you seen it? Have you seen Grace Park? They've already got the foundations down. They've started on the walls. It'll all be finished by Christmas. D'you think they're going to tear that all up because four kids ask them to? 'Course they're not. I bet that Mr Braithwaite never even read our letter except to find out our names. If you don't send it you'll just get into more trouble. What for? For nothing!'

I thought about Mr Braithwaite and Mr Arkwright with their millions of pounds and all their power. And Mr Liversedge who could frighten you just by looking at you. What could we do against them? And anyway, they were smarter than us. They'd fooled us already. In books, all these kids would have got together and outsmarted the adults, but in real life it wasn't like that at all. Perhaps Frankie was right. Perhaps the fight was over. It had been over before we'd even started. And what had we done? Nothing. Collected about four signatures and written a letter that had got me and Trev into a load of trouble.

'Do we just give up, then?'

Frankie sighed. It was as if she had other things on her mind. 'Of course you don't give up,' she said. 'What you have to do is get people on your side. Get public sympathy. That's what they always do. Don't you ever listen to the news?'

I shrugged. 'How do we do that?'

'People have got to hear about it. Get it in the papers or on TV. It may be too late to stop the

Shopping Centre but at least people will know how you feel and that's important. Liversedge, Braithwaite and all those men, they're all the same. The best thing to do is put a bomb under them and their buildings.'

'That's what Grandad said.'

I hoped she wasn't going to suggest I should put a bomb under them.

I said, 'How are we going to get in the papers or on TV? Who'd take any notice of us? We only just managed to get to see the Town Clerk.'

'Remember when the Junior School nearly burnt down?'

I remembered all right. When we'd arrived at school one Wednesday morning the whole of the hall and two classrooms had been burnt to the ground. Two kids from the senior school had poured petrol all over the place and set fire to it. They'd been caught a fortnight later when Ann Markey's parents had heard one of them talking about it in a café.

'Well, that was in the paper for weeks,' said Frankie. 'They even showed pictures of the school on the local TV news.'

I wondered what she was expecting me to do.

'I'm not going to burn the school down.'

'I know that,' said Frankie. 'But you have to think of something like that. Unless you do something really big, everybody will ignore you.'

I wracked my brains. But I could think of nothing.

'Did you see that awards thing on the television tonight?' she said.

'I saw that. Hey, that Australian who made that speech!'

'That's what I was thinking about. That'll be in all the papers tomorrow, won't it?'

I couldn't understand what she was on about.

'You can do the same thing.'

'How d'you mean?'

'In the school play.'

'The one Backhouse is doing?'

'Well, you know it's to open the new Drama Studio.'

'So what?' I said. I didn't see what this had to do with Grace Park.

'Well, everybody will be there. The Headmaster, the Mayor, the newspapers, even the television.'

I thought I could see what she was getting at. 'You mean we could walk up and down as everybody was arriving?' I didn't fancy doing that. I thought how mad Liversedge had been about us going to the Town Hall that time. What would he do if we were to spoil the opening of the theatre?

'No,' said Frankie.

I breathed a sigh of relief.

'Better than that.'

I closed my eyes. I wondered if she was going somewhere I didn't want to follow.

'What you have to do is get a part in the play.'

I looked at her. 'Get a part? What good will

that do? I'm no good at acting, anyway. I hate it.'

'You were acting when I first came to your house.'

Even in the dark it made me blush just thinking about it.

'That was years ago,' I said. 'I was only a kid and anyway that was just messing about.'

'Can't you see it?' she said. 'Out there is the audience. All the most important people in the town; the newspaper reporters, local television. They're all watching the play. The spotlight's on you. Suddenly you stop. That's when you make your speech.'

'My speech?'

'Of course.'

'What speech?'

'Your speech about Grace Park. The play comes to a standstill. You walk to the front of the stage. All the other actors look at you. They don't know what's happening. You look straight out and you say, "Ladies and gentlemen, I'm sorry to stop the play." And then you tell them how awful it is that they're closing Grace Park and about your grandfather and everything.

'Stop the play!' I said.

'Then the next day it will be in all the papers. Can't you see it?' she said. 'They won't be able to ignore it then. The papers will have to print it. They love anything like that. I can just see the headlines. "Grandson of famous Town Player stops the show." You'd be interviewed on the TV

159

News. You might even get on the Wogan Show. They'd have to do something.'

'But you said it was too late.'

She sighed in exasperation. 'I know it's too late but that's not the point. Can't you see? You'd have done something. For Grace Park. For your grandfather. It's a principle. You have to be ready to die for your principles if necessary. I would.'

There was a long silence. I could feel her looking at me. I didn't know if I could do anything like that. She might, but I couldn't. I tried to think of a good excuse.

'They've probably cast it anyway. I saw them having auditions in the hall. It'll be too late now.'

'There's going to be another on Thursday.'

'How d'you know?'

'I was there. Alan Maitland told me.'

'Alan Maitland?'

'I came in at dinner time.'

I was going to tell her about the hole in the glass. How I had hardly recognized her because her hair was long and she'd been wearing a frock. But somehow the words wouldn't come out.

'I didn't see you,' I said.

'No, I didn't stay long,' she said flatly.

She looked at me. 'Is something the matter?'

'No, it's nothing,' I said. I played with the switches on the dashboard. I'd thought of another excuse.

'That play. What happens if I don't get a part? I hate acting. I'm hopeless at acting.'

'You keep saying that. How do you know until you've tried? Of course, if you want to back down. . . '

'Who said I was backing down? I'll probably get expelled, though.'

'No, they wouldn't dare expel you. Not over a principle. If they expel you it just makes you more famous still. You become a martyr.'

'Martyr?'

'Like Joan of Arc.'

I thought about Joan of Arc. Mum had once acted her in a play when I was little. She'd ended up getting burnt to death.

'What I mean is, it isn't as if you were doing it for yourself. That's what principles are. People admire that. They couldn't expel you.'

'What about my mum and dad? They'd go berserk.'

'They'll be proud of you.'

She didn't know my mum and dad. My mum might be all right but my dad . . . ! I tried to think of what he would do to me if I made a fool of myself in front of the whole town. I couldn't imagine it. It was different for Frankie.'

'What would *your* dad do?'

She looked at me sharply. 'My dad?'

'What would he do?'

'My dad couldn't care less. He doesn't care about anything. Except himself. I'll probably never see him again. I don't want to see him again.'

'I thought he was coming back.'

She sniffed and blew her nose. She'd got quite excited while she was explaining the plan to me, now she was behaving strangely once more.

'Of course he's not coming back. You are stupid sometimes. Why can't you understand anything?' She banged with her hand on the dashboard and looked out of the side window. Then she started talking in a low fast voice I'd never heard her use before. She hardly stopped for breath.

'He's not coming back again. Ever. That's why he invited me over. So he could tell me. I thought he was going to tell me that Mum and him were going to try again. Then one day he took me to a hotel. He introduced me to this lady in the foyer. I thought it was someone he was working with. His secretary or something. We went in to dinner. He told me they were going to get married. I thought everybody could hear. Everybody was listening and looking at me. Why did he have to take me over there to tell me? Why couldn't he have told me on the phone? I couldn't look at either of them. I felt sick. I ran out of the restaurant and down the street. They came after me. She was younger than my mum. I hated her. She tried to be nice to me. I hated her more for that. She ironed my dress. I couldn't wear it after she'd touched it. I burnt it. I hated being there. I hated my dad. I never want to see him again. I hate him.'

She looked at me. I couldn't see what expression she was wearing because it was dark. She

162

was knotting her hands. Suddenly she burst into tears.

'I don't hate him,' she said, 'I love him.'

She couldn't speak any more. She didn't put her hands up to her face or anything, she just let the tears fall out. I didn't know what to do. I wondered if I should put my arm round her, but I didn't seem able to. I draped it round the back of the car seat and let it rest on her shoulders. She pulled away from me suddenly.

'Don't do that. You don't understand anything, do you?'

The car was rocking with her sobs. After a time she almost stopped. She took out a tissue and wiped her face.

There was a knock on the car window. Sam looked through.

'What are you doing?' he said.

'Go away,' I shouted.

'What are you doing?'

'Go away!'

'Dad's back. He says, what d'you want for supper?'

'Clear off,' I shouted and pretended I was getting out of the car to bash him.

'Only asking,' Sam said and went out sulking.

Frankie had stopped crying.

'I wasn't crying, really,' she said. 'I was just angry.'

With a little shudder the freezer stopped humming. It was absolutely silent in the garage. I could hear her breathing. We both sat quietly looking out of the windscreen.

'About making that speech,' I said, 'I don't think I could do that.'

She turned and looked at me.

'Is that all you can say? Is that all you can think about? Some stupid park where you used to play stupid football? D'you think that's important? Don't you realize what's happened to me? D'you think I came round just to talk about that? I couldn't care less what happened. You're just like my father. You're just like all men. All you think about is yourself. Except you're not a man, are you? You're a little boy. You're so juvenile. Do what you want. It's nothing to me any more. I've told you what to do. If you're too scared, well, that's your lookout but don't come running to me expecting me to hold your hand because I won't be there.'

She climbed out of the door and slammed it shut with a crash. Then she opened it again.

'Where are those papers?' She opened the glove compartment and took them out. 'I hate this car,' she shouted. She slammed the door again and strode off.

I called after her.

'Who are you calling scared? I'm not scared. You wait, I'll do it.'

But she was gone into the darkness. I think she heard me. I think so, but I couldn't be sure.

I sat there for some time just feeling angry about what she'd said to me. It wasn't like she thought. I had felt sad about her and her dad. I hadn't been able to work out what words to say, that was all. First there'd been Liversedge this morning and now Frankie. Everybody seemed to be getting on my back. If I was going to get into trouble for doing something I might as well do something big and really deserve it. I thought about all the people in the audience all looking up at me. It made me scared just thinking about it.

Dad came into the back yard. He opened the garage door and peered in.

'Benbow, are you there? D'you want this supper or don't you?'

Here was somebody else telling me off. Why couldn't everybody leave me alone?

I climbed out of the car. I didn't feel like eating anyway. I couldn't imagine I'd ever feel hungry again.

I went into the house.

13

That Thursday dinner time I must have stood
outside the drama studio for about a quarter of
an hour, trying to get up the courage to go in. I
hated the idea of going in on my own and everybody staring at me. I tried to persuade Trev to go
in with me. But he wouldn't. He couldn't understand why I was going to audition for *Oliver Twist*
when I'd always said I'd always hated acting.

'You're only doing it because you fancy
Frankie.'

'Don't be stupid.'

'All of them nerks you can't stand will be
there. Maitland, Brian Ogden and Betty Mallard,
uck!'

When he said Betty Mallard's name he made a
noise as if he was being suddenly sick all over the
floor. I don't think *he* liked Betty Mallard, either.
I couldn't tell him about Frankie's plan because I
wasn't sure if I'd be able to carry it out. I wasn't
even sure I'd get a part. I just told him it was to
do with Grace Park but he didn't believe me.

'Why don't we go over the fence one
night and stick a big banner up, then ring
the *Echo* and claim responsibility, like real
terrorists do? Everybody would know about

it but they wouldn't know it was us. Brilliant!'

I had to admit it wasn't a bad idea, but it was too late to turn back now. When he saw he wasn't going to change my mind he got bored and wandered off.

Three kids from the Upper School walked towards the studio. I ran past them pretending to wave at someone on the other side of the playground. I was ashamed that anybody might think I wanted to be in the play. But they didn't even notice me and went in through the door singing in stupid voices. I went back to the door and pushed it open but I couldn't make myself go in. It was as though there was one of those invisible barriers across the doorway. Carlton went past with a couple of other kids. I stood behind this tree so he wouldn't see me. But he did.

'You're not going to audition for that stupid play, are you?' he said.

'No, just waiting for somebody,' I replied.

'Anyway,' he said, 'I'm not supposed to be talking to you.'

'Well, don't then and do me a favour,' I said.

I watched them go. I was almost going to follow them when I had an idea. I was only auditioning for this play to prove to Frankie I wasn't scared, wasn't I? Why didn't I fail the audition on purpose? It couldn't be too difficult to read well enough to convince Frankie that I was trying and badly enough to make Mr Backhouse turn me down. That's what I'd do. I pushed open the door of the drama studio and went in.

It was quite dark, but I could make out the shadows of about thirty kids sitting on the benches and on the floor. I sat in a dark corner where nobody could see me. I looked round but I couldn't make out Frankie. In a bright light on the stage Brian Ogden was doing a scene with Celia Braithwaite. He was supposed to be this character called Bill something or other who's a real villain and Celia Braithwaite was his girlfriend. You could tell Ogden thought he was really brilliant. He kept striding around the stage and pulling faces. Celia Braithwaite's voice was too posh for the rough girl she was supposed to be. After a few minutes I heard Mr Backhouse's voice saying from the middle of the hall:

'Thank you, Celia, that will do very nicely for the time being.'

She jumped off the stage and sat down with the other kids. I wondered if her dad had told her about how we'd charged into his office that time; if he'd read her my letter of apology?

'You stay there,' Mr Backhouse said to Brian Ogden.

A voice next to me said, 'Brian Ogden's g-g-good, isn't he? I think he's g-g-g-got the part already. Mr Backhouse is just hearing other people read who c-c-c-couldn't come to the last audition.'

I didn't need to look round. I knew by the stutter it was Marion Archard. If I'd had a stutter like that I would never have auditioned for a play.

It was bad enough doing it when you could speak properly. I didn't know anything about acting, really, but I didn't think Brian Ogden was very good. He waved his arms around too much but I thought she might think I was big-headed if I said that, so I just said:

'He's not bad.'

My eyes were getting used to the dark by now. I made out Frankie sitting on some steps to the left of the stage. She was whispering to Alan Maitland. I don't think she'd seen me come in. Normally, I'd have gone over and spoken to her, but she'd stormed out of our garage in such a mood the Monday before I didn't know if we were supposed to be still talking to each other or not.

'Are you g-g-going to read for something?' Marion Archard asked me.

'No,' I said trying to sound dead casual, 'I was just wandering past, you know. I wanted to see somebody.' I was trying to sound as if I wasn't really interested.

Frankie was doing the scene now with Brian Ogden. She was better than Celia Braithwaite but she wasn't reading it as if it was real. It was as though she was a bit embarrassed.

'She's really beautiful, isn't she?' Marion Archard said.

I knew she was talking about Frankie.

'Who?' I asked.

'Frankie DeLange.'

'Oh yeah. She's all right, I suppose.'

'I wish I l-l-looked like that.'

Mr Backhouse asked if anybody wanted to read for the part of the Artful Dodger and Kenny Brodie put his hand up. He went up on stage and started creeping around almost bent double and rubbing his hands together, speaking in this weird, croaky voice. He looked like he'd gone mad. It was dead embarrassing. A lot of the kids started giggling. Mr Backhouse stopped him half way through and asked him what he was doing. Kenny said he was trying to be an old man.

Mr Backhouse said, 'But the Artful Dodger is a young boy. It's Fagin who's the old man.'

Everybody laughed even more then. But they were only laughing because they were nervous themselves. I didn't laugh because I knew it would be my turn soon. Even though I knew what I was going to do, I was still nervous. I hate having to stand up and do things in front of loads of people. Like when the teacher asks you to read in class. All the words seem to go blurred and your tongue gets in the way of your teeth and you can feel yourself going all red.

Mr Backhouse asked if anybody else wanted to read the part of Nancy with Brian Ogden and Marion Archard put her hand up. I could tell she was nervous. The bench we were both sitting on was shaking. That's how scared she was. I thought it was going to be terrible if she was that nervous and she had this terrible stutter as well. I was so embarrassed for her I just kept looking at the floor. Then I heard this cockney girl speaking.

I hadn't noticed anybody else going up onto the stage. When I looked up it was Marion Archard. She was putting on this accent. She didn't stutter at all and she hardly looked at her book. When she'd finished her part everybody clapped. She walked away with her head down, chewing her lip, and sat down next to me again.

'I knew I'd stutter if I had to read it so I learned it by heart,' she said. She knew she'd done well. There was a red colour in her cheeks and her eyes were shining.

'Anybody else want to read for Bill?' asked Mr Backhouse.

The bench was shaking again, only this time it was me. I realized I just couldn't face it. I was too scared. Too scared even to do it badly. I crept off the bench.

'Don't you want to do it?' said Marion.

'I have to go to the toilet,' I called back.

Backhouse noticed me creeping towards the door. 'Ah, Benbow, glad you could come.'

'I was just going to the toilet, sir,' I started to say, but he didn't let me finish.

'Up on the stage with you, lad.' He looked round. 'Who else wanted to read Nancy? Betty, you said you did.'

Betty Mallard, I thought. That's all I needed.

As I climbed up the steps to the stage Frankie whispered, 'And don't try and do it badly on purpose, because I'll know.'

I stood on the stage, looking out. The lights were really bright. I put my hand to my forehead to shield them. Betty Mallard was walking up and down getting into the part. Then she suddenly turned and said,

'*I won't scream or cry not once. Hear me. Speak to me. Tell me what I have done.*'

I looked round to see who she was speaking to. 'What?' I said.

Mr Backhouse called from the hall.

'What? What d'you mean, what? Say the lines.'

'What lines, sir?' I asked.

'The lines of the play.'

'I don't know them, sir.'

'They're in the book.'

I could hear Brian Ogden laughing out loud. He was trying to put me off as much as possible.

'He's blind as well as dumb,' he said.

I showed him my fist. 'Shut your stupid face,' I hissed.

'What?' said Mr Backhouse.

'Didn't say anything, sir.'

Betty Mallard whispered loud enough for everybody to hear, 'Just my luck to have somebody who can't read.'

'I can read,' I said.

'Yes, like a dying giraffe.'

Brian Ogden laughed even louder at that. I could hear him whispering to everybody, 'Dying giraffe, I like it. I like it.'

I could feel myself getting mad but I was embarrassed as well. My legs felt as if they were rooted to the spot and my hands had grown three sizes bigger. All my neck and the back of my head felt itchy. I scratched myself.

Mr Backhouse shouted, 'And stop scratching yourself. Look, there are two books on the table. Pick one up, turn to page thirty-five and read.'

I looked round me. There were two tables. I went towards one. I couldn't see any books. I looked underneath and as I did so my shoulder caught the edge and the table collapsed.

I heard someone say, 'It's Clint Eastwood.' Two girls giggled.

I picked up the book from the other table and turned to page thirty-five. Betty Mallard was sitting on a chair looking at the ceiling, trying to show everybody what a hard time she was having acting with me.

'Page thirty-five,' said Mr Backhouse. 'I want you to be Bill. This is the scene were Nancy gets murdered. Start at the top of the page.'

I looked down the page. None of it made sense to me. It was like a foreign language. I couldn't even see 'Bill' written anywhere.

'Have you got it?' asked Mr Backhouse.

'Yes sir,' said Betty Mallard.

'Begin,' said Mr Backhouse.

I didn't know where we were but I didn't want anybody to know so I found the word Bill and just started reading. My plan was going to work whether I wanted it to or not. After this I definitely wouldn't get the part. I thought if Bill was a criminal and a murderer he would have a really rough voice so I started talking in this deep kind of growl. Even while I was reading I heard Alan Maitland whisper, 'Look out, it's Louis Armstrong.'

When I got to the end of the speech I stopped so that Betty could say her part. There was a silence. Betty Mallard was staring at me. I thought maybe she was impressed by my acting.

Mr Backhouse walked to the front of the stage. He clutched his hand to his head and his forehead was wrinkled. He looked like somebody in pain. Really fed up.

'Benbow,' he said in a long-suffering sort of voice, 'why are you reading Nancy's part?'

Everybody was laughing.

'You're supposed to be Bill. Betty is Nancy. Nancy is a girl. Bill is a man. Unless of course you want to swap parts.'

I looked down at my book.

'Sir, there's no Bill here, sir.'

'Does it say Sikes?'

I looked. 'Yes sir.'

'Well, that's who you are, Sikes. Bill Sikes.'

'Ah.'

'Ah. He's got it at last,' said Mr Backhouse, sarcastically. 'Now can we start again, preferably playing the appropriate sexes.'

'Sir,' said Betty Mallard coming to the foot of the stage, 'can I have someone else to do it with?'

'No,' said Mr Backhouse walking away. He waved his hand in the air. 'Let's begin or dinner break will be over.'

I was getting mad by now. Backhouse was

being really sarcastic. Everybody was laughing, I hated Betty Mallard and to top it all I hadn't wanted to read the rotten play in the first place.

I looked to see what Frankie was thinking, but she was saying something to Alan Maitland. She wasn't even looking at me.

I was just about to shout after Mr Backhouse that I hated actors and acting and plays when Betty Mallard started reading.

I don't know if you've ever read this book *Oliver Twist* but it's about an orphan who gets involved with a gang of burglars and pick-pockets run by an old Jew called Fagin. Bill Sikes finds out that his girlfriend, Nancy, has been double-crossing them. He gets really nasty and murders her with his stick and then tries to drown his own dog. I wouldn't have minded drowning Betty Mallard.

Betty started acting. '*It's you, Bill*,' she said in this simpering sort of voice. Everything she did got on my nerves. Her voice, the way she walked, even this trick she had of making her lower lip disappear as though she might cry at any moment. I stared at her.

'It's you now, stupid,' she hissed.

I just lost my temper and pushed her down on to the couch. 'Don't you call me stupid,' I said.

Mr Backhouse looked up surprised. 'That's not in the script,' he said.

Betty tried to get up but I pushed her down again. She slipped off the couch and on to the floor. I picked her up by the top of her blouse and it tore. I heard the buttons falling on the floor.

'Give over pushing, you,' she hissed.

'Get up,' I shouted. I read the lines: '*Leave the light. There's enough light for what I've got to do.*'

Betty Mallard looked really frightened. 'Sir . . .' she said, putting her hand up but I didn't give her a chance. I just carried on with the play. I wanted to get it all over with as quick as possible.

'*You know what you've done, you devil,*' I shouted. '*You was watched tonight. Every word you said was heard.*' I raised my fist as if to hit her with the stick. Betty screamed but somehow carried on with her part. She read it like a robot.

When it was over I just threw the book down and stalked off the stage and sat down on my own. Everybody was dead quiet because I'd been so nasty to Betty Mallard. She was sitting by the side of the stage trying to pull her blouse together. I knew I'd made a fool of myself. I could hear Mr Backhouse's footsteps coming down the hall. He sat down next to me. I didn't look at him.

'Benbow,' he said, 'you astonish me!'

'I'm sorry, sir,' I said. I was, too. I liked Mr Backhouse. He was all right really. But I just couldn't stand Betty Mallard and all her gang making fun of me.

'Sorry?' he said. 'What do you want to be sorry for? There was real anger there. I could feel it even at the back of the hall. I didn't know you had it in you. It just shows what you can do when you try.'

I was really worried. 'Does that mean I've got the part, sir?'

'Well, you don't sound very happy about it. Don't you want to be in the play?'

'No sir.' I saw Frankie was listening. 'I mean, yes sir.'

'Good,' he said. 'Well, I've got to hear some other people but for sheer energy that reading's going to take some beating.'

I looked up. Brian Ogden was watching us. I raised my eyebrows at him as if to say, it wasn't my fault that I'd got the part. He looked really mad.

Mr Backhouse said, 'Couldn't you speak up a bit, Betty? Benbow wasn't getting very much help from you.'

Betty's eyes flashed. 'Sir, he was shouting at me all the time. Look, my blouse's ripped.'

'That's exactly what he's supposed to do. I think we'd better see Marion do that part again.'

Betty Mallard stormed off the stage giving her book to Marion. She looked straight at me. Her eyes were narrow and her mouth a tight little circle. 'You!' she spat out and walked away.

I just smiled.

On Friday there was a notice up in the front corridor. At the top it said *Oliver Twist* and underneath was a list of the characters and who would be playing them.

Alan Maitland was Fagin, Frankie was Mrs

Bedwin, Marion Archard was Nancy and against the part of Bill Sikes was written my name. I looked up and down the corridor and read it again. Four times. I'd never been picked for anything before. I didn't know what to think. In a way I was pleased, even though it had all been a mistake. But on the other hand I would have to carry out Frankie's plan. There was no avoiding it now. That's what happens when you lose your temper, I thought.

I read my name again and thought of everybody else seeing it up there on the board. Even though I was on my own I couldn't help smiling.

14

Out of the darkness they looked up at me.
Three hundred pairs of eyes. They were all
there; Braithwaite, Liversedge, Grandad. All of
them. I knew what I had to say. I had the words
ready. I opened my mouth but it wouldn't move.
No matter how hard I tried it wouldn't open. I
looked round for my mum. She'd know what to
do. I heard Grandad's voice saying, 'She's not
here you know. She's not here.' I looked out
but I couldn't see him anywhere. His seat was
empty. I shouted, 'Grandad' but no sound came
out. Everybody stood up and put their coats on.
They started to walk away. They shouldn't leave
yet. I tried to hold them back, but it was as though
I wasn't there. Frankie would know what to do.
She was running up the broad steps at Grace Park.
I tried to follow but I could hardly move my legs.
The harder I tried, the slower I went. She was
there now, on the cliff. The wind blew her hair
about. Long hair in the wind. She mustn't jump.
It was so high and there were rocks. She was
gone. I looked over the edge and she was floating
down. Alan Maitland caught her and they started
laughing. It was funny how they flew across the
sea. The edge of the cliff was crumbling. I tried to

struggle back but I couldn't get my feet to move. The cliff fell away. And I was falling. Falling for ever and ever . . .

I woke up with my heart pounding and my body drenched in sweat. For a moment I didn't know where I was. Then I saw the sunlight shining through my bedroom window. I hadn't had a nightmare for years. I suppose I was worried about the play and having to do my speech. At 7.30 I'd be walking on to the stage, saying my lines. Just thinking about it made me go all funny inside. I thought, if only it was a normal Saturday morning and there was no play to do, the six of us would have gone down to Grace Park. Three months ago I'd taken it for granted. Hadn't thought it was anything special. Now I'd have given anything to have been able to turn the clock back. But nobody seemed interested in playing football any more. Trev said it was because Grace Park had disappeared under brick and concrete, that it wouldn't seem right to play the World Cup anywhere else. But it was more than that. There was nothing to stop us having a kick around somewhere else. It didn't have to be Grace Park. Everybody seemed to be doing different things; drifting apart. I was in the play; John Stokes had bought a racing bike and had surprised himself and everybody else by being good at it. He raced for a local club and spent all his weekends training. He was mad on cycling and even wore those shiny black pants and racing gloves in school. Carlton's mum had banned him from even talking to us because she said I was a bad influence. And Frankie. Well, I never saw much of her now. Although we were in the same play we seemed to rehearse on different days and when we did rehearse together we hardly ever talked. She spent most of her time with Alan Maitland's crowd: Brian Ogden, Celia Braithwaite and them. They were all older than me. Everything seemed to be changing. So that left Trev and me. And since I'd got a part in the play we didn't seem to be getting on too well.

After I'd had my breakfast I decided to ring him up. We arranged to go over the rec for a kick around. We'd call on Frankie on the way. See if she wanted to come. It would be like old times. But it didn't work out like that. About a hundred yards from Frankie's house we saw her coming out with Alan Maitland. At first I didn't recognize her. She had her hair all done on top and was wearing these high heels. I was going to try and walk past as if I hadn't recognized her but, of course, Trev had to go and wave. When he did that I pretended to be really surprised but I think he saw through me.

Trev said, 'You know she's going out with him.'

I said, 'Don't be stupid.'

I'd never thought of that; of Frankie going out with lads. A year ago she'd have made fun of anybody doing that and, somehow, I'd thought it would be me. I felt sick.

I bounced the ball on the pavement.

'Want to come for a kick around later?' I shouted at her.

'Not today, Benbow, we're going to Rushworth & Draper.'

Rushworth & Draper was a big music shop in town. Lots of kids went there on Saturday mornings and listened to records through headphones but never bought anything. She waved and went on down the street.

Of course, Trev had to say, 'I told you so.'

I pretended to drop the ball so I could watch them. At the corner near Jackson's they stopped. Maitland was saying something to her. She put her hand on his arm. It must have been something stupid because she started laughing. This daft laugh I'd never heard her do before. And then they disappeared round the corner. Trev was waiting for me.

'Told you she's going out with him.'

Trev's my best mate but sometimes I could kill him.

'Shut up you,' I shouted.

'You're only mad because you fancy her yourself.'

'Don't be daft,' I said and started thumping him. Every time I met Trev these days I seemed to end up thumping him or having an argument with him. In the end he took his ball and went home. We walked all the way down Linaker Lane shouting insults at one another until we were out of sight. We never got to the rec that day. Trev and me didn't talk to each other for about three days after that. I didn't seem to have any friends any more. I began to wonder if there was something wrong with me. Trev started chalking these stupid signs over the pavement. A heart with an arrow through and mine and Frankie's initials. That made me even madder because I thought Frankie might think I'd done it. I went round for days rubbing them off with my foot. She probably didn't care what I thought so I was probably wasting my time.

A fortnight earlier, at one of the rehearsals, something had happened that made me realize how much she'd changed. Mr Backhouse had kept us on at rehearsal after school until nearly eight o'clock. Sometimes Frankie'd come and talk to me, but it was only to ask me about my mum or my grandad or something like that. If I wanted to talk to her I had to join in with her group, which I never liked because they were always making jokes nobody else could understand, and I didn't think were funny, anyway. I felt I didn't belong there. Brian Ogden was still mad that I'd got the part of Bill Sikes instead of him and took any opportunity he could to make me feel stupid. He was always talking in this old-fashioned English, saying things like 'zounds' and 'eftsoons' that everybody thought was hilarious but I thought just sounded stupid. Anyway, this time, when they were all grumbling at how long the rehearsal had gone on for, Betty Mallard said, 'I think this rehearsal is going to go on for ever and ever.'

I looked at Frankie and said our old catch phrase,

'And for ever is a long, long time,' and laughed. But nobody else joined in, not even Frankie. She didn't even smile. It was as if she couldn't remember any of those things we'd done in the past. I felt really stupid. After that I didn't try to speak to her if she was with the rest of her gang. I sat on my own or with Marion Archard who could be quite funny when you got to know her. She was really good at imitating people. If you didn't look at her you'd think it was them. She laughed at my jokes, too, which is more than the rest of them did.

It was awkward not being able to speak to Frankie, because I wanted her to help me work out the speech I was supposed to be making. That was the only reason I was in the play, for a start. But once I'd got the part she never mentioned it and whenever I tried to bring it up she'd change the subject. I supposed she was doing it on purpose; trying me out, seeing if I'd do it without any help from her. I thought, I'll show her. I'll show her I can do it without any help from anybody. I'd decided to do my speech on the first Saturday of the play. That's when all the important people, the Mayor, the Town Clerk, the local newspapers would be there. I planned to do it just before the interval so that they could talk about it while they were having their drinks. I thought if I did it at the end they'd all just go home and forget about it. I tried to give myself courage by pretending it wasn't really important. I always do that. It's only acting, I said to myself. It's only standing up in the dark in front of a lot of strangers, wearing somebody else's clothes. It was a daft carry-on really. In two hundred years' time it'd all be forgotten. But it didn't stop me worrying. It was the most frightening thing I'd ever done in my life. To make it easier for myself I'd learned the speech as if it was part of the play. Then I'd do it automatically, without thinking. I thought that was the best way. In this scene Oliver Twist is practising stealing handkerchiefs. Fagin calls them 'wipes'. Oliver just thinks it's a game. He doesn't realize they're practising how to steal. Fagin comes down to Oliver and puts his arm round him. He brings him down to the front. *'You're a good boy, ain't you, Oliver?'* Then he turns to me and says, *'Don't you think he's a good boy, Bill?'* And I was supposed to say, *'He'll do, Fagin.'* Because I'm planning to use him in a robbery. Fagin understands what I'm thinking about and winks. Then he says, *'What do you say, Bill, what do you say?'* And that's where I was going to come to the front of the stage and make my speech.

It sounds funny but even when I was just rehearsing that bit I could feel myself getting more and more nervous. Of course, I never did it in rehearsals. That would have given the game away. But I got nervous all the same. Quite often I forgot my words there.

Backhouse said, 'I can't understand you, Benbow. You're word perfect in every other part of the play but you always get lost there. Is something the matter?'

I knew what the matter was. So did Frankie. But I wasn't going to tell anyone else. It was funny that Frankie and I knew what was going to happen and nobody else did. They just carried on with the rehearsal. They didn't know the terrible thing I was going to do. Thinking about that made me feel really strange. Like I did when I was about nine and used to walk around pretending I was a secret service agent who was going to blow up the whole town in five minutes' time. I'd look at all the people going to the shops or gardening or catching buses and think, they don't know that in five minutes they'll all be dead. I was the only one who knew that. Well, that's how I felt about doing this speech. All I could see was me walking out to the front of the stage and saying this speech. Even though it hadn't happened yet I could see it all as clear as anything. The faces looking up. The people on the stage shifting about and nervous. It was like a dream. Only it was a dream that was about to happen. Anything could trigger my fear off. All anybody had to do was mention anything to do with the play and I'd see it all happening clear as anything and my heart would start beating like mad. Like, my mum would say, 'Have you learned your lines yet?' Something like that and the dream would come into my head. Or Mr Allen, who took us for technical drawing, would say as he looked at my work: 'Just because you're playing Bill Sikes you don't have to draw like him.' It was a joke. But I couldn't laugh. This fear got in the way.

Something else was happening. I couldn't say when it started. It just sort of crept up on me without me realizing it. I was starting to enjoy being Bill Sikes. I think I must have been quite good at it. I don't know why, because I'd never acted before. I'd always thought I'd hate it. But as the rehearsals went on I started to feel at home on the stage. That's the only way I could think to describe it. It was as though I'd always been there. As if I'd always done acting. I liked being Bill Sikes. I suppose that was what it was. I was happy being somebody other than myself. I was able to believe in what I was saying. The words just came out sounding natural, not as if they were in a play but as though it was really happening. It was funny. I wasn't being big-headed but I kept thinking to myself: this is something I can do! Something I'm good at. That had never happened to me before. I'd never been any good at anything else really. Not even football. I could play all right and I liked it but I was never really good. Not good like Grandad must have been when he was young. Even Frankie said to me once during rehearsals, 'You know, you're really good as Bill Sikes. Something happens to you. Your face changes and the way you walk. I think maybe you were always an actor. Even when you played football you were always good at looking like a footballer but you could never really play.'

It was funny being good at something for the

first time. For one thing it made all the things I was bad at, like maths and physics, seem less important. I'd always looked at other lads and thought: they can do maths or play the piano or bowl fast. I'd wonder what it was like to be able to do something like that really well. I'd look at these lads and wonder where it was that skill came from. Why couldn't anybody do it? And now *I* could do something. It was as though suddenly I'd become someone else. A stranger I was just getting to know. It was funny.

Alan Maitland didn't like it. He kept saying to Backhouse, 'Sir, couldn't you get Benbow to say that bit quicker?' or 'Sir, couldn't I come on a bit later?' Alan Maitland took it all really seriously. But Backhouse never took much notice. Later on I found out why he wanted to do well in the play. Why he wanted to be noticed. There was going to be a big production of *Oliver Twist* in the Grand Theatre in Town and they wanted lads to play the young characters. Of course they had professional actors to play the older people. Mr Backhouse told us at one rehearsal that they'd be coming to one of our performances to see if any of us were any good and that in the Christmas holidays they'd be having more auditions. I knew Alan Maitland was dead keen to get the part of Oliver. He was always talking about acting and films. He knew the names of all the actors. I wasn't really bothered. Mum knew one or two people she'd acted with in the past. She'd point them out whenever we saw them on the telly. 'Oh, there's so and so,' she'd say. 'He had terribly bad breath. It was terrible if you had to kiss him.' Things like that. But I never told anybody else about it. The worst thing was knowing that after I'd made my speech nobody would ever want to talk to me again. I'd be a leper. Nobody would ever want me for a play again. It would be like being sent off in a football match. Red card for Benbow. I was scared all right. But if you wanted to do something important you had to make sacrifices. Frankie said so.

It was Saturday night. I sat in the dressing room with all the rest of the lads looking at my face in the mirror. There were tables round all the walls with little bulbs above them so you could see properly to put your make-up on. I'd never put make-up on before. Miss Slaney showed me how. She rubbed black stuff all round my chin to make it look as though I hadn't shaved. It didn't look like a beard at all to me. Just like a dirty smudge but Miss Slaney seemed pleased. When she'd gone I rubbed it off again. Everybody was talking and laughing a lot. That's because they were nervous. I kept thinking that they didn't know what I was going to do. It was a terrible secret that I carried around inside me. I almost thought they could tell by looking at me; that somehow it showed on my face. But I knew that couldn't be possible. Mr Backhouse came in and wished everybody luck. I think he was more nervous than we were. He kept asking if there was anything we wanted. Some lads were quite cheeky. Barney Tasker asked for a glass of orange. Backhouse didn't seem to mind. He went off and got it for him. When he came back, he said there was a full house. I went into the wings at the side of the stage. I could hear this murmur of conversation. Every now and then somebody would cough or laugh loudly. There was a little gap in the curtain. The hall was full. I could see Mr Liversedge in the front row. Mr Braithwaite was there, too. And I could see Grandad and my dad in the third row. My mum wasn't there, though. There was an empty seat. Perhaps she was late. Even though I was going to mess up the play, I couldn't help being really nervous. My legs started to feel all weak. I began to think of all the places I'd rather be. I wished I was sitting out in the audience. It made you feel really funny to think that all these people had come to see us. Mr Backhouse put his hand on my shoulder.

'Just do what you've done in rehearsal, Benbow, and you'll be marvellous.'

'Yes sir,' I said.

A load of lads trooped past and took up their places on the stage for the workhouse scene that opened the play. I wasn't on for a bit and neither was Frankie.

'Sssh,' said Mr Backhouse. Everybody went quiet. 'Stand by,' he said and stuck his thumb up towards the lighting and the sound bay. I looked out through the gap in the curtain. I could see my grandad laughing. Then he seemed to be disappearing. The lights started to go down and the audience stopped talking. The music began. I knew it really well by now. It was funny to think the audience was hearing it for the first time. Then the play started.

The audience seemed to like the play. They laughed a lot and clapped. I hadn't thought about them doing that. All the things I'd stopped laughing at, I found interesting again. Just like I had when I'd first heard them. At the end of the first scene the curtain went down and the audience clapped. I saw Frankie on the other side of the stage. She was talking in a whisper to Alan Maitland. He looked at me but I pretended not to see. I started to think about my first line. I couldn't remember it! I thought: I'm going to go out there and not be able to say anything. I won't be able to remember a word. Then from nowhere the words came back to me.

'*Fagin you're an avaricious old fool.*' That was the line. I kept repeating it over and over to myself so I wouldn't forget. I didn't know what the second line was. If I started thinking about that I forgot the first line. I just hoped it would come out of my mouth at the right time.

The second scene was over. It was our scene next.

'*Fagin, you're an avaricious old fool.*' I repeated it three times to myself in a whisper. The words were starting to lose their meaning. Like they do when you say the same word over and over again. I started thinking about the word *Fagin*. What did it mean? I'd forgotten he was a character. My heart was beating so loudly I could hear it thumping in my ears. My mouth was dry. I wouldn't be able to speak. I tried to swallow but I couldn't.

Somebody was at my shoulder. It was Frankie. I thought she was going to wish me luck. She didn't look at me, at all. We both stood there watching the scene shifters setting out the furniture.

Frankie said suddenly, 'I don't want you to do it.'

I was so lost in fear at doing the play that at first I didn't know what she was on about. Mr Backhouse was lifting a table on his own. The audience was talking in whispers.

'Do what?'

She still didn't look at me. 'I don't think you ought to do that speech.'

I looked at her. She was biting her lip.

'You can't change it now,' I said.

'It wouldn't be right.'

'You suggested it,' I said. 'It was you came up with the idea in the first place.'

'I know. It's my fault but I just know it would be wrong.'

Half of me was relieved. I'd always been led by Frankie. If she said not to do it, I thought, maybe it was all right. Alan Maitland was watching us. I knew I wasn't going to do it but I pretended that I was.

'I can't change my mind now. It's too late. I've written this speech.'

'You mustn't do it.'

'Why?'

'Lots of reasons. Everybody's put a lot of work into the play. It wouldn't be fair to them. Two wrongs don't make a right.'

'But you knew that before.'

She paused. For the first time she looked at me.

'If I was to tell you there was a better way.'

'Better? Than the speech?'

'Yes. Would you not do it?'

I pretended to be thinking about it. But I'd already decided I wasn't going to do the speech.

Mr Backhouse came over. 'Ready?' he said. 'Ten seconds.'

'Have you got an idea?' I whispered to Frankie.

She hesitated. 'Yes,' she said.

'A good one. Better than the speech?'

'Much better.'

'You're not just saying that?'

'The scene's beginning. I'll tell you later.'

'Promise?'

'Cross my heart.'

Mr Backhouse shooed the scene-changers off the set.

'Ready,' he said in a whisper.

Frankie put her hand on mine. 'You won't do it, will you?'

Frankie had never asked me a favour before. I didn't know what to say.

The curtain was about to go up.

'I don't know,' I said.

'Please,' said Frankie. She ran away and took her place on stage.

The curtain went up. A feeling came over me starting at my feet and rising slowly to my head. It was like that time when Dad had given me a glass of champagne last Christmas. I didn't have to make the speech. I could have sung out loud. I looked on stage. Frankie was saying her line. I'd be on soon. I realized I was still frightened. Maitland was on. He had a false beard and wore a dirty old gown. I pulled up these mittens I had to wear and tightened the ragged scarf round my neck. I'd be out there soon, saying my line. My line? What was it? I listened to Fagin talking to the gang. But the words sounded hollow and far away, as though something had happened to my hearing. What was my first line? Something about Fagin and then that big word. What was it? I heard my cue coming up. Automatically I walked on stage. The lights were hot. I couldn't see the audience but I could feel them out there. I knew I mustn't look at them. I stopped thinking. I was Bill Sikes. I felt a sort of hardness behind the skin of my head. Like Bill's violence wanting to break out, to break out of my skull. I couldn't think what I was supposed to say. My brain had stopped working. I wasn't even sure where I was any more. I heard my cue. I tried to think of the line. What was it? The more I thought the less it would come into my head. It seemed as though the silence lasted for hours. Everybody must know. They all must know I'd forgotten my first line. I wondered why the prompt hadn't said it. My legs were shaking. Then, somebody said it. Someone else on stage said my line very loudly. I wondered who it was that was imitating my way of talking. But nobody seemed to notice. They just went on with the play as if everything was normal. I realized it must have been me who'd said it. I'd opened my mouth and the right line had come out. I decided not to think. Thinking didn't help anything. The play went on.

15

It was the airship that gave me the idea. It
was floating and bobbing like a huge silver cigar
over Grace Park as I walked home from school
with Trev after school on Monday night. Trailing
from the back of it was a long banner on which
was written in large red letters:

OPENING AT EASTER.
THE ARKWRIGHT SHOPPING PLAZA

That's what they were going to call Grace
Park when it opened. Even the name would
be changed. Like Grandad said, by the time
they'd finished there wouldn't even be a smell
left behind. It would all have disappeared.
Everybody who went past in their cars or
on buses craned forward to read what it said.
You couldn't miss it. It was a brilliant adver-
tisement. But it made me mad to see it. If I'd
had an airgun I'd have shot it to pieces there and
then.

'Don't be stupid,' said Trev, 'the skin would
be too thick. Anyway you'd never reach with an
airgun. Too far away.'

Trev was deliberately looking on the black

side because he still bore a grudge from Saturday. I pretended not to mind because I wanted us to be mates again. I stared up at the sign. You could see it for miles around. It was then the idea came to me but I pretended it was Trev's. I knew it would make him feel better.

'Hey, man,' I said, 'that idea you had about putting up a sign, why don't we hang it on the balloon?'

I could tell he was flattered but he still had to keep a bit of the grudge going.

'How would we get up there?' he said. 'Catch me climbing up a wire that long.'

'You don't have to climb up it. It's on a kind of winch. They had one at the school fete last year. We bring it down, tear off their message and put our own up.'

It wasn't as good as stopping the play, I knew that, but it was something. I could see Trev liked the idea but he couldn't allow himself to be enthusiastic too soon.

'What's the use? They've nearly built the place,' he said.

'That's not the point. It's the principle.'

Trev looked at me. 'Did Frankie teach you them big words?'

' 'Course not,' I said.

Before he could say anything else I said, 'We'll do it tomorrow night. After midnight. If you don't come I'll do it on my own. What you say, man?'

He seemed to look at the advert for a long time before he nodded his head. 'Tomorrow night,' he said. He thumped me on the shoulder and smiled. I thumped him back. We were mates again.

It sounds stupid, but I felt I'd let Grace Park down by not doing my speech the Saturday before. I wanted to make up for it. After that it would be over. I didn't even know for sure that the wire was attached by a winch. It didn't really matter. We could always hang it on a couple of trees. The important thing was to do *something*.

During the Tuesday dinner break we sneaked into the drama studio and painted our message on a long piece of cloth that had been used as a bit of scenery in another play. When we held it up it was fifteen feet long. On it was written:

REMEMBER GRACE PARK

in bright red lettering. We rolled it up and on our way home from school left it behind a shed near the Park. We arranged to meet at two o'clock.

That night I didn't set the alarm clock in case it woke everybody up. I went to bed with all my clothes on and kept the curtains open so I wouldn't go to sleep. All the time though, I was on the edge of falling asleep. I had to keep pinching myself and moving my head and arms and legs about to stop my eyes from closing. A couple of times I even got up and walked round the bedroom. Even so, I still fell asleep. I don't know what woke me up. I looked at the clock. It said one o'clock.

I crept out onto the landing, closing the bedroom door softly behind me. The landing light had been left on. I thought, that'll make my dad mad. He hates people leaving the electric on. I'd just reached the top of the stairs when a man in a blue uniform came out of the bathroom. He just walked past me as if it was the most natural thing in the world and went downstairs. I stared after him and wondered if I was still dreaming. Then Mum came running up the stairs in her dressing gown. There wasn't time to hide. I tried to think up an excuse but I didn't get a chance. All she said was, 'Go back to bed. I'll tell you about it later.'

Then my dad ran up the stairs and into their bedroom. He came out after a second with a blanket. He said to Mum, 'This one'll do, they're ready to go now.'

Sam came out rubbing his eyes and I heard Baby Andrew crying. Mum took Sam's hand and led him back to his bedroom. I couldn't understand it. There I was, standing fully clothed at one o'clock in the morning and nobody was saying anything to me. I didn't know what to do or what was going on. Dad said, 'Sorry we woke you up. Make yourself a drink, we'll tell you about it in a minute.'

I didn't want a drink. I didn't know what to think. I wondered if there'd been a fire or we'd been burgled. Just my luck it should happen on this night. Whatever it was, I hoped it would soon be over so that I could get down to Grace Park. I thought of Trev waiting for me by that workman's shed and then getting fed up and deciding to go home.

After about a quarter of an hour my mum came in. When I heard her I jumped back into bed as quickly as I could and pulled the blankets over me. I didn't even take my boots off. She sat down on the edge of my bed. Her eyes were red and there were dark patches underneath.

She said, 'It's your grandad. He had another attack in the night. They've had to take him to hospital. Dad's gone with him.'

I just looked at her. I didn't know what to say. 'Is he going to be all right?'

'I don't know. I think so. I hope so.' She was nearly crying. 'He's had these attacks before. He's come through. He's a fighter, is Grandad.'

What I was thinking was that Grandad was Mum's dad. Like my dad was to me. It was funny to think of her being five or six and Grandad being her dad and taking her to school. I'd never thought of her being little before. I mean I knew she had been young once but I'd never thought of it in the same way.

'You try to get to sleep.' She patted me on the head. I felt as if I was about four again. After she'd left I lay for a few minutes in the darkness. I kept thinking about Grandad. How he'd be going through the night in the ambulance; and then in the hospital with a lot of people who didn't know him. I could see him telling this sister how he'd scored the goal that had put the Town into the

Final. If it hadn't have been for Trev I would have stayed in the house. But I had to go.

The house was dark. I felt my way down the stairs, through the kitchen and out through the back door. The light in Mum's bedroom was out. There was no one about.

When I reached the outskirts of Grace Park I had a job finding the shed. Everything seemed different in the dark. There was no sign of Trev. I called softly but there was no answer. If he didn't turn up after what had happened to Grandad, I'd kill him. I'd only come out so as not to let him down. I tried to find the banner. It wasn't there. Somebody must have found out about us. I crawled on all fours along the side of the shed and eventually felt the material under my hand. Where was Trev? I looked round. My eyes were getting used to the dark by now. The ten-foot-high netting was still there but in places there were walls made of wood. They would be impossible to get over. I tried my foot on the netting. I could just about get my toe in. The wire cut into my hands. It was hard to believe that there had once been a football ground there. That thousands had roared with joy to see my grandad score the goal that had put mighty Everton out of the Cup and taken the Town on to the Final. For a moment, in the darkness, I could see Grandad as he'd been in that newspaper photograph; proud and youthful with his hair combed back and the old-fashioned boots.

I heard a sound in the bushes. I knew there was

a watchman on duty all night. A figure came out of the darkness. It was Trev. We talked in whispers.

'What kept you?'

'I've been here ages. I thought you weren't going to come. I was just going to go home.'

'My grandad was ill. They had to take him to hospital.'

I told Trev about the stranger in uniform coming out of the bathroom, and how I'd got back into bed with my boots on. Any other time we'd have laughed about it but tonight we were both too frightened to find it funny.

'Where's the sign?'

'By the shed.'

We crept back to the shed and carried the sign up to the wire fence. It wasn't heavy but it was awkward. We looked up at the fence. It seemed to disappear into the darkness. As if it went on for ever.

Trev said, 'You're going to have a job carrying this up that fence.'

'What you mean *me*?'

'Well, I can't climb over, can I?'

'Why not?'

'My leg, man.'

'What about your leg?'

'I've hurt it, haven't I? Anyway it's your turn. I went over last time.'

'What last time?'

'Before, when the dog went for me.'

I'd forgotten about the dog. It started to drizzle. I thought about how warm and safe my bed would be. Trev seemed to read my thoughts.

'Shall we go home?' he said.

For a moment I almost agreed with him. Then I thought of my grandad. The sooner I started, the sooner it would be over.

I wrapped the end of the sign round my waist.

'Feed the rest up to me. When I get to the top of the fence let go and I'll drop it down the other side.'

'What happens if someone comes?'

'Whistle.'

'Whistle? They'll know where I am then.'

'Like an owl.'

'An owl?'

I thought of all the films I'd seen where Indians broke into forts and camps in the middle of the night. I cupped my hands round my lips and blew.

'That sounds more like a wolf than an owl.'

I put one foot into the wire netting and started to climb. In the commando films I'd seen, they seemed to fly up fences and roll over at the top. But I could hardly get the toes of my boots into the mesh and my arms weren't really strong enough to pull myself up. My hands were cold and the wire cut into them. After about five minutes I'd climbed four or five feet.

'Get a move on,' said Trev. He was dancing up and down trying to keep warm.

The worst part was trying to swing myself over the top. It wasn't steady like a wall but swayed from side to side and shook as you tried to get your body over. I pulled up the slack on the banner and dropped it on to the other side. Going down was easier than going up. I jumped the last three feet, landing on all fours in the mud. Suddenly the clouds cleared and the moon sailed out.

I rolled up the banner and crept across to where I thought the airship would be. At last I saw it, floating black against the moon. I couldn't find the rope that tethered it. I suppose the wind must have blown the airship away at an angle. In the end I fell over it, barking my shins. I ran my hands along it. It wasn't a rope. It was a thick wire hawser and it was fixed to the ground with bolts and plates. It would be impossible to pull the ship down. It had all been a wasted journey. I might as well have stayed in bed. I looked round. I wasn't going back without hanging the banner somewhere. A tree would do.

It was then I heard the dog. I didn't wait to see it but turned and ran as fast as I could in the direction of the fence. I fell sprawling over a coil of wire. The dog was nearer now. He was making the strangest noise. It wasn't like a bark. Just a long held sound that went on and on. I wondered if Trev could hear it. Then I saw the dog, large and black, racing round one of the JCBs. The fence was about fifteen yards away. I dragged myself to my feet but the banner had caught in the wire. I pulled it free and stumbled for the fence, the banner trailing on the ground behind me. The dog was almost on me.

'What's happening?' shouted Trev. I didn't

answer. I was too busy trying to get a foothold on the fence. The dog was right behind me snarling and slavering. Desperately I flung myself up. Something was pulling me down. I thought, my leg! 'He's got my leg!' I screamed. On the other side I heard Trev shouting with fear. I was being pulled down. I looked back. The dog was on his hind legs. His front paws were up against the fence. His eyes looked red in the light and his lips were drawn back. I felt myself falling. He had hold of the banner and tore at it, jerking his head violently sideways. I let go the banner. The dog fell back, rolling over and over, the banner wrapping round him. It gave me time to regain my hand hold and climb up and onto the top. The dog was up and snarling at me again. Then I was over and falling. I heard the crack as I landed.

I was swimming. Swimming on a huge black lake. As far as I could see there was water. Black water. But I wasn't scared. I wasn't worried about anything. I could swim for ever. A voice was calling. Calling to me from somewhere I couldn't see.

For some reason I only seemed to have one arm. It didn't worry me. Nothing worried me. The empty sleeve trailed behind. There was that voice again. Nearer now. I could make out the words. I must be nearer. 'Over here,' the voice said. There was a small island. A young man was standing there. He was waving me over. The top of my head was warm with the sun. I could see the man clearer now. 'Over here.' It was Grandad. He was young. Just like he'd been in the photograph. I was glad he was all right. I would tell him how easy it was to swim even with one arm. He'd like me to tell him that. Now he was well and young we'd play football together. I loved my grandad. I'd never told him that. It was a good time to tell him. He looked down at me. He was smiling. He held down his hand to me and began to pull me up out of the water. I looked round. I liked the island. Grandad would be happy there. I was glad he was happy. That sun was hot, though. Right in my eyes it shone. My arm was beginning to ache again. Perhaps I'd better not play for a bit. Just lie down. That was it, just lie there. But the sun was hot. I told him that. I told him the sun was hot.

The doctor said, 'That's it, you keep talking.'

The sun was a lamp. It was burning in my eyes. I put my hand up to shield them but it was hard to move my hand. It was heavy. It was very heavy. I touched it with my other hand. It seemed to have got thicker and harder. It was heavy with plaster. I looked round. My mum was standing by the door. The room was all white. I asked them where Grandad was and what had happened to the island. Mum came over. She laid her hand on mine.

'You were dreaming,' she said. 'The doctor gave you an anaesthetic so he could set your arm.'

'All right, sonny?' asked the doctor. He held

up his hand and spread out his fingers in front of my face.

'How many fingers can you see?'

I counted them.

'Three,' I said.

'How many now?'

'Four,' I said.

The doctor nodded, 'Good job he fell on his arm. He could have fractured his skull from that height.'

Then it started to come back to me, like a story I'd half forgotten. I remembered the dog and how I'd fallen off the fence. I wondered about Trev.

'I drove you both to the hospital, then put him in a taxi.'

Mum helped me into the car. 'I shall have to ring his mum when we get home,' she said.

'Don't tell anybody about this.' I pointed at my arm.

'What do you mean? Don't tell anybody? They're bound to know. They only have to look at your arm.'

She put the seat belt round me.

'Don't tell Trev my arm's broken.'

'Why ever not?'

'I don't want him to know. I don't want anybody to know. Just say I fell.'

We turned out of the hospital entrance. It was just getting light. People were standing at bus stops and walking to work. A milk float rattled by. On the way home Mum told me

what had happened after I'd fallen off the fence.
Trev had walked home with me and knocked at
our door. At first, Mum had thought it was Dad
coming back from the hospital. She'd left a note
for Dad and driven straight round to the Casualty
Department. I'd fallen on my left arm and broken
it just below the elbow. It was a clean break. I
thought about my arm. It was aching. The plaster stopped just above my hand and there was
a bandage under my thumb. My fingers looked
very pink against the white of the plaster.

'What day is it tomorrow?'

'It's already tomorrow. Wednesday.'

I moved my arm gently and wondered if I'd
be able to do the play.

'Will you be coming Saturday?'

'I'm in Birmingham on Saturday. I've a part in
The Archers. What's important about Saturday?'

She'd forgotten already. 'The last performance
of the play.'

She looked at me. 'If you think you're going
to act in a play with a broken arm you've another
thing coming.'

'Why not? *You* did.'

'When?'

'You said. You broke your wrist once and
Dad didn't want you to do it. You said the
show must go on.'

'That was different.'

'How was it different?'

'I'm not going to argue with you. You can't
act with a broken arm.'

'I don't act with my arm.'

If Backhouse found out, he might stop me doing the play. He'd probably get Brian Ogden to do it using the book.

'You're not to tell anybody about this,' I said.

'What d'you mean, don't tell anybody? They're bound to know.'

'No they won't. The plaster stops above my hand. And, anyway, Bill Sikes wears these gloves.'

'I've said no and that's an end of it.'

'If I don't do it they might have to cancel the play.'

'Don't argue.'

'I'm going to do the play and nobody's going to stop me.'

'Why, for heaven's sake? What's all this desperation to do the play suddenly?'

I thought about it. I wasn't quite sure.

'It's a question of principle,' I said.

Mum glanced at me. She started to say something, then stopped.

Principle seemed to be a useful word. It stopped people talking.

'We'll have to see. I'll talk to your dad. See what the doctor says.'

When she said that, I knew she'd let me do it. If ever she said, I'll have to think about it, you knew you'd win in the end.

Mum yawned and turned into our street. It was a shame I couldn't tell them at school. It would make a good story. Trev would have enjoyed it.

In five minutes it would have been all round the school with all his usual exaggerations . . . 'Anyway, this huge dog jumps over this twenty-foot fence but I managed to get him to the ground and get both hands round his throat when suddenly . . .' I'd keep it till after the play. We stopped outside our front door. The light was on in the kitchen. I wondered if my dad was still up.

'Anyway,' said my mum, 'what were you doing there in the first place?'

With me breaking my arm and having to go to hospital she'd forgotten to ask why I'd been out in the middle of the night falling off fences. Now she knew I was all right and wasn't going to die she started to get angry. 'What were you doing climbing over that fence in the middle of the night? You were thieving, weren't you? My God, I bring you up the best I can and this is what you do. This is the thanks I get. Didn't you think? Didn't you stop and think for one second about what you were doing? I've had enough of a shock tonight with Grandad, without having this happen. Getting woken up at three in the morning. You looked like a ghost. When I think of you on that fence. Falling all that way. You might have killed yourself . . . What would I have done? We'd have lost you, darling.'

She sobbed and hugged me tight to her. I could feel her tears crawling down my face. 'You could have been lying out there in the rain and I wouldn't have known.' She hugged me harder. It hurt my arm.

'Ouch,' I said.

'Oh my darling, your poor arm.'

Then she started shouting at me again.

'Well, it's your own fault. You've no one to blame but yourself. If you hadn't gone out thieving, you wouldn't have fallen off. Serves you jolly well right. What are we going to do? My God, we've got a thief in the family. It's my fault. I shouldn't have done those plays when you were a baby. I should have stayed at home where you needed me. Your father was right. I've neglected you. I've been a bad mother. I don't want you to grow up to be a criminal. How could you do it to me? How could you?'

She punched me hard on the shoulder. I winced.

She put her arm round me. 'Darling, your poor arm. Are you all right? Oh love, did I hurt you? Oh I am sorry.' And she started hugging me and crying all over again.

I thought about the banner lying in the mud.

'I wasn't stealing,' I said. 'We weren't taking anything away, we were trying to take something in.'

And I told her everything.

It was five o'clock when I got into bed. At eight someone pulled me awake. It was Sam.

'Can I have a look at your plaster?'

I pulled my arm from under the bedclothes. He looked at it solemnly for three or four seconds.

'You can't do acting with that.'

'Who says?'

'I heard them arguing about it. They're going to ask the doctor.'

'They're not going to stop me.'

'You say.'

I hit him gently on the head with the plaster. Bonk, it went.

'Ow,' said Sam, 'that hurt.' He rubbed his head. 'Did you really fall off a fence?'

'Jumped,' I said. 'Not fell, jumped.'

'Why?'

I thought about that. Why had I done it? It was difficult to explain. I didn't really understand it myself.

'You wouldn't understand,' I said.

'Would. Would understand.'

I sighed. I could feel my eyes closing. At least the banner was on the right side of the fence. That was something. I supposed some workmen would find it covered in mud and wonder what it was all about and then throw it into a dustbin. But it hadn't been a waste of time.

'Principle. It was a principle,' I said.

'A principle?'

He nodded his head as if he understood what I was talking about.

'Is that why you've got a day off school?'

'That's why,' I said.

I think Sam might have asked some more questions. But I couldn't remember. I fell asleep and didn't dream.

16

It was the last performance of the play and my arm was beginning to ache. I couldn't carry it in the sling while I was on stage. Most of the time I hooked my thumb into my overcoat pocket. But it still hurt. We were just coming up to the interval. It was the scene where I'd planned to do my speech. Only now of course I wouldn't be doing it. There was a period in this scene when I didn't have much to say; just had to stay in character; stand still and look interested in what was going on. My arm throbbed. I was dying to shift it but I couldn't in full view of the audience. The pain was making me feel sick. I had to do something. I walked to the back of the stage and pretended to gaze out of the window as if I was watching something in the street. With my back to the audience I eased my thumb out of my pocket and tucked the broken arm into the front of my overcoat. It was more comfortable there. Alan Maitland's eyes followed me. My moving had put him off. He hesitated and then said some lines back to front. For a moment I thought he was going to stop altogether but he managed to carry on. When he'd finished his bit he came over to the window like he was supposed to. The Artful Dodger and the rest of the gang were teaching Oliver how to pinch handkerchiefs. There was a lot of noise going on at the front of the stage. Alan Maitland glared at me.

'What you bloody doing up here? You're not supposed to be up here. You're supposed to be down there. Have you gone mad?'

I couldn't tell him about my arm.

'I felt like a change.'

'You felt like a change?' He looked really mad. I could see he was sweating behind his make up.

We were both speaking in whispers out of the corners of our mouths and had our backs to the audience.

'You know they're out there, don't you?'

'Who's out there?'

'Them. The people from the Grand. You mess this up for me and I'll kill you.'

'*Let's you and me talk about it,*' I said loudly. It was a line from the play. I was supposed to say it but it took Maitland by surprise. I strode off stage and into the wings. Miss Slaney was standing there. She clapped her hands silently and beamed.

'It's going awfully well,' she whispered. 'I love the new move you've introduced where you both stand at the window.' She gave me a funny sort of pat on the shoulder. She hadn't noticed what had been going on. Neither had the audience. I suppose they didn't know what was supposed to happen so they wouldn't know when anything went wrong, unless it was really obvious.

214

Maitland came off after me. As soon as he was out of sight of the audience he grabbed me by the coat collar.

'I'm warning you, Benbow. You go on messing this up and I'll . . . What d'you mean by going to the window when you're not supposed to?'

I hadn't been trying to mess it up at all. It was just that my arm had been hurting. But I wasn't going to tell him that. I tried to take his hands off my coat but I could only use one arm and anyway he was much bigger and stronger than me.

Miss Slaney who was on the curtain looked at us anxiously.

'Stop that,' she hissed, 'they'll hear you.'

On stage Dodger and his pals were running around shouting and laughing. Frankie was in the wings on the other side of the stage watching us. Maitland took no notice of Miss Slaney.

'I know what you were planning on doing.'

'What you mean?'

'Making that speech.'

'What speech?'

'I know all about it, Benbow. You think you're so bloody clever, don't you?'

'Boys, boys, please!' said Miss Slaney, looking round anxiously, but Maitland carried on.

'Francesca told me all about it.'

'Francesca?'

For a second I didn't know who he was talking about and then I realized.

'Frankie told you?' I said. 'I don't believe you.'

215

'She told me you were going to stop the play for some stupid reason.'

'It wasn't a stupid reason.'

On stage it had gone quiet. Our cue to re-enter had been said but Maitland was so busy going on at me that he hadn't noticed it.

'Don't you think of doing anything like that,' he pulled me up by the coat until his face was an inch away from mine. 'Don't you even think about it. Or else.'

He drew his fist back threateningly.

The gang on stage were looking anxiously in our direction.

Mr Backhouse came running over. 'What is going on?'

Maitland still had me by the coat. I shrugged. There wasn't much I could do.

'*Here come Fagin and Bill now,*' said Dodger for the second time. They all looked hopefully in our direction.

Alan Maitland started to explain. Mr Backhouse was shaking with anger.

'Don't explain anything,' he hissed. 'Just get on that stage.'

Maitland let go of me and we walked onto stage. The lights blinded me. I was in a turmoil. Frankie! Frankie had told *Maitland*! Had told *him*! I couldn't believe it. It was nothing to do with him. It was her and me, that was all. Just her and me. She'd told me she had another plan. A better one. But it wasn't true. She'd lied to me. Made it all up just to stop me doing the speech.

It was because of Alan Maitland. He must have asked her to and she'd done what he'd told her.

While these thoughts were racing through my mind I was still saying my lines. It was funny to think I was standing in a bright light in front of two hundred strangers thinking about anything but the play and yet the right words kept coming out of my mouth, almost automatically.

I looked at Fagin.

'*You can believe the girl, Fagin, can't you? You've known her long enough to trust her. She's not one to blab.*'

It was a line in the play but I said it like I'd never said it before. Very sarcastically. I really meant it. Maitland looked at me. He knew I was talking about Frankie, too. Behind his false beard and make-up I could see he was really worried. I got the feeling that he had no idea what I might do next. We were getting close to the interval; approaching the point where I'd intended to do my speech. I suppose he was worried in case I might still do it. He had this idea that I was unpredictable. Perhaps he was right. I thought, if he's *that* worried I'll really give him something to worry about.

Nancy brought in a bottle of beer for me and laid it on the table.

'*You're a good boy, ain't you, Oliver?*' Fagin said, patting Oliver on the head. He tried to say it with a laugh in his voice but he couldn't keep it from shaking.

I picked up the beer. I was supposed to pour it into a glass but I couldn't because of having my arm in plaster, so I just picked up the bottle and pulled out the cork with my teeth. It felt better like that. It was what Bill Sikes would have done. I could see Frankie watching me from the wings. I wondered if she might be worried that I was going to do the speech. For a second it flashed through my mind that I might. But it didn't last long. I spat the cork out. It sounded like a paper bag bursting. Alan Maitland's head jerked round in surprise. His eyebrows were going up and down and there was a sort of panic in his eyes. He was one of these actors who liked to do everything exactly the same every night. If you changed a word or a move he went mad and started to forget where he was in the play. He'd noticed I'd drunk out of the bottle and not out of a glass and I could see that it had upset him. It was my line. I kept him waiting. I thought, I'll frighten him a bit more. I only had one more line to say before the interval. I had to say, *'He'll do, Fagin. Oliver will do.'* Then Fagin had another line and the curtain came down. I usually said my line by the table. That's what he was expecting. But I walked over to him. I could tell by the look in his eyes that he didn't know what might happen next. His pupils were dodging from side to side. I handed him the bottle of beer. He clutched it. His eyes had gone glazed.

'Have a swig, Fagin,' I said.

Maitland looked over towards the prompt.

Frankie was there standing next to Mr Backhouse. He had his hand to his head and his mouth was hanging open. They both knew what was supposed to happen in the play. They must have thought I'd gone mad. Maitland swivelled his eyes round and stared at me. Then he looked down at the bottle in his hand as if he didn't know where it had come from.

'*Knock it back, Fagin,*' I said.

Maitland nodded like someone in a daze. Then he lifted the bottle and drank from it.

'*He'll do, Fagin,*' I said. '*Oliver will do.*' That was my real line.

When I said the right line, relief flooded over Maitland's face. He knew where he was. He took the bottle from his lips and said his line. But his mouth was still full of water. He half swallowed, tried to get the words out but started choking instead; choking and coughing and spitting water all over the stage. Somehow between the coughs he got the line out while I patted him on the back. More water came out and the curtain came down. The audience cheered and laughed. They were probably thinking what a brilliant actor Alan Maitland was to make all that coughing look so natural. But he wasn't pleased. He was still coughing. He came over towards me his eyes streaming. I thought he might thump me but another coughing fit seized him and he had to go off. He was red in the face and shaking his fist at me.

Frankie was angry too. She said, 'What d'you

think you're doing? That was Alan's best bit in the play and you ruined it.'

Mr Backhouse raised his finger at me. 'Stick to the text, Benbow.'

I was nobody's friend. I didn't care. I shrugged my shoulders and went off to the dressing room. I sat down in front of the mirror and looked at my face. My eyes were bloodshot from the make-up. I didn't look much different from the real Bill Sikes. I thought, I shouldn't have done that really, it might have ruined the play, but something inside me had made me do it. I couldn't fight him so I got back at him in the only way I could. It was a way of getting back at Frankie, too. Anyway, you could say I'd done him a favour. The audience had liked all the coughing at the end. But I didn't suppose he'd see it like that. I looked hard at my face. It was funny but I could hardly recognize myself. It was like looking at a stranger. Like in one of those horror films where your body gets taken over. My face was white. Even through the make-up it was white. There was a funny acid taste in my throat and mouth and my arm was aching badly. I suddenly realized I was going to be sick. I rushed into the toilet and slammed the door behind me. After I'd been sick I felt better. But I stayed there kneeling down getting my breath back.

I heard Mr Backhouse calling out. 'Five minutes. Five minutes till the second half, everybody.'

Brian Ogden came in with Billy Parrish who

was playing the Artful Dodger. I didn't want anybody to know I was sick. I locked the door quietly.

I heard Billy saying, 'D'you see what Benbow did?'

Brian Ogden was whistling. He stopped. 'No, what?' he said.

'He walked over and gave Maitland a drink.'

'Isn't he supposed to?'

'Is he heck as like. It made him choke. He's really mad. They nearly had a fight.'

'On stage?'

'No, when they went off. He'll bash Benbow when he catches him.'

I didn't care if he did bash me. I really didn't care what happened. I felt like going out and saying, here I am. If he wants to bash me go and get him. But I heard Billy Parrish say something that made me turn to ice.

'Maybe Benbow's a bit funny because of his grandad.'

'What about his grandad?'

I stopped breathing.

'Didn't you know?' said Parrish. 'He died in the hospital this afternoon.'

'Died?' said Brian Ogden. 'Does he know?'

' 'Course not. My sister works at the hospital. I heard her telling my mum at tea-time. They didn't tell him because of the play.'

I heard them going out. The door closed. I was lying on the floor.

Why hadn't they told me? They should have

told me. He was *my* grandad. Everything was very clear all round me. All the colours bright and hard-edged. Grandad dead. I didn't understand what it meant. Did that mean he wasn't coming back? I tried to think of him lying in hospital. Very still with his hands across his chest. But I couldn't. I couldn't cry either. The door of the dressing room opened. I heard footsteps. I didn't want anybody to find me there. Mr Backhouse's voice said, 'Has anybody seen Benbow? God, where is he? The curtain's about to go up.'

I heard Brian Ogden say, 'I haven't seen him, sir.'

'Oh Lord, where is he?'

I heard him walking towards the toilets. 'Nobody in the toilets, is there?'

I kept quiet.

They went out and I heard the door of the dressing room slamming shut and their voices disappearing down the corridor. I came out of the toilet and stood there in the middle of the room. I felt as though my body didn't belong to me. For a second I thought of running away. Running across the playing fields; running anywhere until I couldn't run any more and never coming back. But then I thought, where can I go? Wherever I went to, my grandad wouldn't be there. I thought, that's what it meant to be dead. Grandad was somewhere where I couldn't find him. That wherever I looked I wouldn't find him. Ever.

I walked towards the stage. They were all in their places, waiting for the curtain to go up. Mr Backhouse saw me. He came over and tried to get hold of my arm to pull me onto the stage.

'Where have you been? I've been looking all over for you. Don't ever do that to me again.'

I just walked past him as if he wasn't there. Just kept on walking and took up my place on the stage.

'Well, never mind now. Just get on with the play,' he whispered and hurried off into the wings gesturing to Miss Slaney and the lighting man that we were all ready.

I looked round at everybody else on the stage. Frankie and Marion Archard and Alan Maitland. They didn't know. For them it was just an ordinary day. Just like any other. Afterwards, they'd go home and their grandads would be there. And they'd ask them how they'd got on. I looked round at the set. It felt good being there. I thought it would be good to be on a stage like this all your life. Everything always happened as you'd rehearsed it. People died and then they got up again and bowed to the audience. They smiled and bowed at all the people. But out there past the cricket field and the rugby posts, down Station Road where the hospital was, they didn't get up. There was no audience to bow to. I felt I wanted to stay on the stage and never get off. It was all right here. It was safe.

The curtain went up. It was funny, I didn't think about anything except the play. In a way

I wasn't even *thinking* about it. I was the play. I knew I was on a stage and that there were people out there watching, but it was as if I didn't have to think about what I was supposed to do or say. I somehow didn't have to try. It just all happened. I could tell that the audience knew it as well. They were really quiet. They didn't want to miss a word. There was a part in the play where Bill Sikes has to try to drown his dog because he's afraid someone might recognize it and give him away to the police. Of course it wasn't a real dog. I had to put some stones in a handkerchief then try to tie them round the dog's neck before throwing him into this pond. But the dog doesn't trust me and runs away. Whenever I'd done it before I'd done it as though I didn't care. I just wanted to catch him and drown him. When he runs away I was supposed to shout and curse after him. That's how Mr Backhouse had wanted it. He told me that Bill Sikes was a hard, cruel man. He wouldn't have thought anything about killing a dog. He was a murderer. But when I came to that part I held the dog as if it was real. There was water splashing on my hands. I was crying. I was crying real tears. It was strange. I was cradling this toy dog and tears were pouring out of my eyes. Then I threw the stones and the handkerchief away and cursed the dog. I was swearing and crying all at the same time.

When the play ended the audience wouldn't stop clapping and cheering. They even stood up and held their hands above their heads and clapped. Everybody on stage was excited and kept laughing and bowing. They raised and lowered the curtains about ten times. Then I thought of my grandad. I thought, I shouldn't be laughing. I shouldn't have cared about the play. I could see the faces of the audience. They looked red in the light. Their eyes were shining. I wondered what I was doing at the front of the stage. I hadn't noticed myself walking there. I looked back. All the other actors were looking at me. The audience went quiet and sat down. They looked up at me as if they expected me to say something. I heard a hissing noise. Mr Backhouse was gesturing me to get back in line from behind one of the curtains at the side of the stage. I looked round at the other actors. Then at the audience again. It was very quiet. I knew I had to say something.

I said, 'My grandad . . .' I stopped. What was I supposed to say. My head was buzzing. I coughed and looked at the floor. I tried to think of the speech I'd learned but I couldn't remember one word of it. The audience were still looking at me. I tried again. 'My grandad . . . you see . . . well they shouldn't have . . . they shouldn't have done that . . . not Grace Park . . . That's where he scored . . . and . . .'

The words wouldn't come out. I knew what I wanted to say but I couldn't make any sense of the words. The people listened. I don't think they knew what I was on about but they listened. Then I stopped. I stopped and just stared out at them. The silence seemed to go on for a long time. Then suddenly they started clapping. I don't think they knew what they were clapping for. Maybe they just felt like clapping. Or perhaps they were feeling sympathetic. I didn't want anybody to feel sorry for me. That wasn't why I'd done it. Mr Backhouse walked out and stood beside me. He put his hand on my shoulder. We walked back together into the line. All the others were looking at me. Maybe they thought I was mad. I didn't care, though. I thought about the hospital. In my mind I could see it, with the lights of the wards burning all night.

Then the curtain came down.

In the dressing room, everybody was shouting and laughing. Alan Maitland took his make-up off on the other side from me. I could see him watching me in the mirror. He wouldn't do anything while we were in the dressing room. Anyway, I didn't care. I didn't care about anything. In a funny sort of way I almost wanted him to go for me; wanted something to happen. Mr Backhouse was over the moon. He went round to everybody, patting them on the back and saying how good they were. Even Miss Slaney came in to say how good we'd all been. Billy Parrish was running around in his underpants. She pretended to be embarrassed and covered her face and said she was sorry. I didn't speak to anybody. Even when Mr Backhouse came over and said how he'd liked the way I'd done the bit with the dog. He even asked me if I'd ever thought of going in for acting. He said if I wanted to he'd give me a reference. But

I couldn't answer. All I did was nod. My mouth was all dry. I thought maybe I'd never speak again.

Mr Backhouse leaned over me. His breath smelled of tobacco.

He said, 'Is everything all right, Benbow?' There was a long pause. I looked at him and then carried on wiping off my make-up. I could see he knew about Grandad but he didn't know if I knew. He just nodded and patted me on the shoulder. It jarred the arm I'd broken but I didn't show anything. He went off to speak to somebody else.

All this time I could see that Alan Maitland was watching me. I knew he'd be mad because I'd made him look a fool. He was the sort of kid who hated to look stupid in front of people.

All the time I was getting dressed I kept thinking about my grandad; that all afternoon I'd been at my Auntie Denise's house, cutting her lawn. And while I'd been walking up and down behind the lawn mower Grandad had still been alive. And then at a certain moment he'd stopped breathing and I hadn't known about it. I hadn't know that he'd died. Later, Auntie Denise had come into the garden. She'd had this funny expression on her face. She said my mum had phoned to say I was to have tea at her house and to go straight on to school from there. Now I knew why.

I picked up my things and walked out without saying goodnight to anybody. As I closed the door I heard somebody saying, 'It's because the play's over.' But it wasn't that, at all. You could always do another play. Doing another play was no problem.

I didn't want to go home. I walked down Roe Lane carrying my bag in my good hand. A double-decker bus went past. It was going near our house but I didn't want to catch it. None of the people on the bus knew that my grandad was dead. It didn't matter to them. I wanted to cry but I couldn't. I had this feeling that I was letting Grandad down by not crying. The gates on the railway line were closed. A train came through. Some people got on. They were going to London. Riding through the night. It would be nice to get on a train and get off somewhere completely different, where no one knew you. Start a new life. But I couldn't see beyond what happened after I got off the train. The train pulled out. I watched it until it was out of sight and then carried on walking. I didn't care where I went. There was a blaring sound and a voice shouted out, 'Why don't you look where you're going?' An ambulance zoomed past. I looked up. I was outside the Cottage Hospital. That's where they'd taken Grandad. I wanted to look in through the window into the ward where he'd been when I'd last visited him on Friday. I'd gone on my own, on my way home from school. It was round the side. I don't know why I wanted to see it. I just did. I felt I couldn't go home until I had. I walked across the grass and round the side of the building. I slipped on my knees in the mud.

There was a small one-storey building. That was the one. The door swung open and two nurses came out, laughing. I hid behind a car until they'd gone. There was a row of windows down the side. Something made me want to look through. Perhaps I was half expecting to see Grandad there; sitting up in his bed reading. Or in a seat with his head down, sleeping. I'd go in and say, 'Hello, Grandad,' He'd look up and say, 'Benjie'. And then start telling me one of his stories. I wouldn't have minded hearing one of them again. I tried to think of what was the last thing he'd said to me. Somehow it was important that I should remember. People always remembered last words. He'd been asleep when I'd arrived. I'd sat at the side of the bed looking at his face. Then he'd woken. He hadn't looked surprised to see me there. It was as though he was expecting me. We talked about the play and what I was doing at school then he'd asked me to look in his drawer. Between the pages of a book was the faded newspaper photograph of Grandad kicking a ball. Underneath it said

Benbow's late winner takes Town to the Final

'I wanted you to have that,' he said. I folded it carefully and put it in my inside pocket. He was very short of breath.

'Did I ever tell you how we came to get to Wembley?'

'No, Grandad,' I said.

And he started to tell me the story I'd heard a thousand times before but he fell asleep in the middle of a sentence. I sat there for a few minutes looking round. A lady had come in wearing a big hat. She'd come to visit the man next door to Grandad. He was very yellow looking, and there were tubes coming out of his nose and into his arm. The lady pulled the screens round them. Then I heard Grandad calling. I looked up. He beckoned me to go to him. I went and stood near him. I bent my head down because he spoke very quietly.

He said, 'Are you all right for a bob or two?'

I said, 'I'm all right, Grandad.'

'Pass me my purse.'

I fetched his purse out of the drawer. He took it from me and opened it. His fingers were bent and there were brown and yellow spots on them.

He reached inside and took out a fifty-pence piece. He pressed it into my hand. 'That's for your bus fare,' he said.

As last words go they weren't great but I was glad I'd remembered.

Through the window I could see all the beds laid out. An old man in a dressing gown was walking slowly down the middle of the room. Where Grandad had been the bed was empty. There were a lot of empty beds. I turned and ran off as fast as I could, jumping over the low wall down Scarisbrick New Road past the Co-op and all the building work near Grace Park until I came to the shops a couple of roads up from our street. Somebody shouted from the darkness of one of the shop doorways. He shouted my name. I stopped. Two figures came out into the light. One kept walking towards me.

'What you want?' I called.

'What do you think?' said the figure. He came closer. It was Alan Maitland. He kept walking slowly towards me. I didn't try to run away. When he was about five yards away he stopped.

'I've been waiting for you,' he said.

I didn't say anything. I hoped he couldn't see the plaster on my arm. I thought, if he sees I've got a bad arm he'll be more likely to hit me. I held it behind my back against the wall.

He came right up to me. The other figure said, 'Come on, Alan, leave it.' I recognized Frankie's voice.

'Just a minute,' he said to her, 'I've got something to sort out.'

He looked at me.

'What was all that about?'

'All what about?'

'You know. In the play. Giving me that drink. Trying to make a fool of me.'

'Wasn't trying to make a fool.'

'Come off it, Benbow. Don't give me that.'

I didn't know why I'd done it. It had just happened. I'm like that sometimes. Sometimes I just do things without knowing why. In a way I was sorry. But I wasn't going to tell him that. I just kept looking straight into his eyes. I'd read somewhere that that was what you were supposed to do if a mad dog attacked you. It showed you weren't afraid, even if you were.

'Alan, come on,' Frankie said.

He half looked round. 'We're just having a little talk, that's all.'

'If you're not coming, I'm off,' she said. But she didn't move.

Alan Maitland took another pace towards me. 'You know why you did it. You can't stand anybody looking good except yourself.'

That wasn't true either. I didn't tell *him* though. I just kept looking. I wondered if he was going to hit me.

'You knew all those people were there. You knew they were looking for somebody for their play.' He thumped me on the shoulder. As soon as he did that I knew he wasn't really going to hit me. If he had been going to beat me up he'd have started straight away. The only reason he would hit me now was if I tried to hit him back. As long as I just kept looking at him and doing nothing he'd get fed up and go off. He might thump me a few times on the shoulder or in the arm but he wouldn't beat me up.

'You think you're so good, don't you, Benbow? You think you can do what you like.'

'Come on, Alan,' said Frankie from the shadows. She came forward and took hold of his arm. I looked at her for a moment and then back at Maitland. He shrugged her off.

'Alan, please,' she said.

232

'I just want him to apologize. Just say he's sorry. You just say you're sorry and we can all go home.'

There was a silence.

'Well? Are you sorry?'

I shook my head. 'No,' I said.

He got hold of my shirt collar and pulled me up towards him. All his mouth was twisted. Suddenly he was yelping and holding his leg. I hadn't meant to kick him. It was when he'd caught hold of me I couldn't help my foot going up and into his shin. It was a bad move. I'd done it in front of Frankie. Now he'd have to hit me. He came towards me with his fist raised. Frankie tried to stop him but he pushed her. She fell to the floor.

'You've asked for it now,' he said.

He pulled his fist back. Instinctively I held up my arm to protect my face. There was a terrible crack and suddenly I was back against the wall and sliding to the floor. There was blood coming out of my nose. I struggled to my feet getting ready to avoid the next blow. But it never came. I heard a moaning sound. Alan Maitland was bent double cradling his hand.

'My hand,' he kept mumbling, 'you've broken my hand.'

I realized he'd hit my plaster with his fist. He'd hit me so hard it had fractured his hand. My arm had bounced back and crashed into my face. That's why my nose was bleeding. I didn't wait to find out how bad he was hurt. It was his fault anyway for trying to hit me. What for? For nothing. For giving him a drink on stage. That was all.

Frankie came over to where I was lying. She tried to help me up. I pushed her away.

'Benjie,' she said, 'I'm sorry.' She held out a handkerchief.

'Leave me alone,' I shouted. 'You told him, didn't you? You told him. Why don't you all leave me alone?'

I got to my feet and started stumbling down the road.

I heard Frankie shouting, 'Benjie, wait.' But I wasn't hanging about. His other fist would still be sound. I could taste the blood in my mouth. It was trickling down my throat. I stopped to spit into the gutter. I heard a noise behind me. I thought it was Alan Maitland and started stumbling on towards our house. Lights swept across me and a car stopped.

I tried to hide in the shadow of a tree. The car door opened and footsteps clicked towards me.

'Benjie.'

It was my mum. I looked up.

'What have you been doing?'

I looked at her and wiped the blood off my lip.

'Nothing,' I said.

'Nothing?' She looked at me half frowning and half smiling. 'I see. Fine. Well, if it's nothing you'd better get in the car.'

I tell you one thing about my mum. She accepts everything you say. If I'd said 'Nothing' like that to a teacher at school they'd have gone on and on about it. But Mum never did. So I usually told her everything. But not tonight. I didn't want to speak to anybody, really.

I got in the car.

'D'you want a hankie?'

She pressed a small white handkerchief into my hand. I dabbed at my nose. It smelled of perfume.

'I hit myself with my plaster.'

'Sounds like a sensible thing to do,' she said.

She put the car into gear and pulled away. I looked back through the rear-view mirror but I couldn't see Maitland or Frankie.

There was a long silence. Mum glanced at me a couple of times but she didn't say anything. I guessed she was thinking about Grandad. I was thinking about him, too. She wasn't sure if I knew or not.

We turned the corner into Lakey Lane. People were drifting out of the Odeon.

Without looking at me, Mum said, 'You surprised me tonight.'

'What do you mean?'

'I thought you were really good. That bit with the dog. Where you shouted at him and then pretended to cry. I almost believed it was real.'

'I wasn't pretending,' I said.

'I could never do that. Cry on stage. I had to have an onion in a hankie. What a fraud.'

That was interesting.

She went on. 'Some people can do it. Some can't. There was one actor I was in a play with – when the director asked him to cry he'd say, "Which eye?" '

She'd told me that before. Last time, though, it had been an actress. But I didn't say anything.

'It's a gift, crying. I tried everything. Thought of the saddest thing I knew. But no go. I didn't have the gift.'

We pulled up in front of the house. She switched off the engine and turned the lights out. We didn't get out. Just sat there staring straight ahead. The car creaked and made funny little cracking sounds. There was a light on in our front room.

'That's what I did,' I said.

'What?'

'I thought about Grandad.'

I'd told her now. It was out. She shifted in her seat and sighed. I thought maybe she was going to cry. Or put her arm round me like she'd done before. I wouldn't have minded. I'd have liked it. But I couldn't tell her. I knew she was thinking the same as me.

I said, 'I didn't know you were at the play. I thought you would be too busy to come. You're always busy.' I was trying to make it sound as though I was talking normally. But it came out sounding funny. As though I was sulking.

Mum looked at me. 'I wouldn't be much of a mother if I was too busy to see our Benjie in a play, would I?'

I knew she'd tried to make it sound jokey but it came out funny.

She was sniffing.

She said, 'Can I borrow my hankie back? Got a bit of a cold.'

I handed her the handkerchief.

'There's blood,' I said.

'Thicker than water,' she said.

She blew her nose. And pressed the hankie into my hand. She clung on to my hand and didn't let go. I could feel her fingers flexing. I didn't let go either. We sat there for a long time not saying anything. Just staring straight ahead.

Then she said, 'Looks as though that might be our house. Coming in?' We got out and locked the car and walked into the house.

17

One Saturday morning, about six weeks after the play had finished, there had been a ring at the front door. I was lying on the carpet in our front room playing Monopoly with Sam. It wasn't much fun playing Monopoly with Sam because whenever he started losing he used to cheat like mad. He never used to be like that. I supposed I still liked him because he was my brother but he was changing. Before, he used to do everything I told him, maybe because I was bigger and he was a bit scared of me. Now he argued about everything. My mum said it was a stage he was going through. I just hoped it wasn't going to last very long. The game was getting to that point where he only had to land on my property once and it would be all over. I had hotels all down the right hand side of the board and if Sam threw a three or a five he was going to land on Mayfair or Park Lane. He rolled the dice out of the egg cup but instead of it landing on the board he made sure it went on the carpet where I couldn't see.

'Twelve,' he said, 'two hundred pounds, please,' and just snatched it out of the bank.

'It was never twelve,' I said, 'let's see.'

But he wouldn't and dropped the dice so he

wouldn't have to show me. Then he accused me of not playing fair.

The door opened and Dad was standing there in a striped plastic apron.

'Someone to see you,' he said.

Frankie came in and stood in the doorway. I wondered if I should get up or not and decided not to. A year ago I wouldn't have had to think about it. I found I couldn't look at her. I just kept staring at the Monopoly board and pretending we were at an important stage of the game. My dad went out.

After what seemed like an age, she said, 'Playing Monopoly?'

Well, it was obvious we were. If it had been the old days, before she'd stopped playing football and started going out with Alan Maitland and everything, I'd have probably said something dead sarcastic like, 'No, we're skinning a dead cat.' But I knew it wouldn't be appropriate to say that now.

Sam picked up a Chance card from the middle of the pack. 'Bank error in your favour collect two hundred pounds,' he shouted and he made crowd cheering noises with his mouth. 'Wish all this money was real.'

'Everybody says that,' said Frankie. She was trying to be friendly. I hadn't spoken to her since the last night of the play when I'd had that fight with Alan Maitland. I'd seen her round school but whenever she looked as though she was going to come up and speak to me I'd walk off in the other direction. I sneaked a look at her. She was wearing tweed sort of trousers and a jumper with small bits of glass stuck over it. Her hair was nearly down to her waist. She was wearing two rings. She'd never worn rings before. She looked about seventeen. Almost like a different person. I thought it was funny how people could change in such a short time. First Sam and now Frankie.

She looked at me. I was embarrassed that she'd caught me looking at her so I looked away quickly but I knew she'd noticed.

'Who's winning?' she asked.

'I am,' I said.

'No you're not,' said Sam. 'I've got lots of money. Tens of thousands of billions of trillions of zillions of pounds.'

He was showing off because Frankie was there. He showed off all the time. He showed off even when he was on his own.

Sam threw all the money up in the air. It fluttered down over the sofa, the window sill, the carpet and the piano.

Frankie said, 'He's going to be a gangster when he grows up.'

I thumped Sam gently on the shoulder. 'Who says he's going to live long enough to grow up?'

Sam started yelling and clutching his shoulder.

'He hit me. Dad, he hit me.'

Dad shouted from the kitchen. 'Sam, come here and help with the washing up.'

'No,' said Sam sticking out his lower lip. He went out, slamming the door. I could hear his voice from the kitchen saying over and over, 'He hit me, Dad, he hit me. Ben hit me.' Dad made soothing noises.

I was sorry he was gone. It was more embarrassing being on my own with Frankie. I started to pick up the notes. Frankie walked round the front room looking at everything as if she'd never been in there before. She picked up a photo of Mum taken from a play she'd been in.

'Your mum still acting?'

I coughed. 'Yeah. She's working today.'

'What is she doing, a play?'

'No, it's an advert for local radio. Woodland's Furniture Store. She has to come out and say what a bargain she got in loose covers.'

'That's interesting.'

It wasn't interesting at all, really. We both knew she was just making conversation.

She knelt down on the carpet and started helping to pack the game away.

I folded the money neatly. If anyone had looked through the window they would have thought we were competing in a Duke of Edinburgh Tidiness Award.

'How's your arm?' Frankie asked.

I rolled up my sleeve. 'Took the plaster off. Nurse came at me with these huge curved scissors and an electric saw.'

'Yeah, I know. I had plaster on my leg when I was seven. Terrifying.'

'Yeah.'

'Alan's had his plaster off too.'

She'd said it quickly without thinking. She realized it was a mistake to have mentioned Alan and the fight I'd had with him.

I pretended nothing had happened. I spoke as casually as I could.

'Did he get the part at the Grand?'

Frankie put the lid on the Monopoly box.

'No. But there's another show at Christmas. *Hiawatha*. They're going to be auditioning during the Easter Holidays. He might try again.'

I knew then she was still seeing him. She realized it, too.

She said quickly, 'You going to go in for it?'

'I don't know,' I said.

She was looking out of the window. I rippled through a pile of hundred pound notes. They made a rustling sound.

'Sorry about your grandad. I didn't know. Alan didn't know, either.'

I didn't say anything. Thinking about my grandad upset me.

'Did you go to the funeral? What was it like?'

I thought about it. The church had been near my old primary school. As they'd lowered the coffin into the grave, two crows flew out of a tree. Across the rugby pitch you could hear the children singing *The Grand Old Duke of York*. We used to sing that in Mrs Roberts' class when I was there. Mum was hanging on to Dad's arm. Grandad's coffin had looked very small.

'It was all right,' I said.

'You liked your grandad, didn't you?'

I nodded.

There was another long silence.

She sat down next to me on the sofa. She handed me a piece of paper.

I looked at it.

There were typed questions and dotted lines left for you to write.

In one of the spaces somebody had written, R. R. Wilson, RIBA.

'Who's Wilson?' I asked.

'It was my mother's name. Before she got married. She's passed her architects' exam. I've to take this to O'Reilly's. They'll get this written in brass for her so she can put it outside her door. I'm going there now.'

I didn't know why she was showing me this.

'You want to come along?'

'Where?'

'O'Reilly's. That's where they do it. By the canal. It's nice there. Might be interesting.

I thought about it. 'I dunno,' I said. I was wondering if Alan Maitland was going. I didn't want to meet him.

'Alan's gone to his uncle's. In Harrogate.'

I wondered if she'd said that because she'd known what I was thinking. She took the paper from me and folded it. 'Better than doing nothing,' she said.

She was trying to be friendly. I thought I might as well go.

On the bus we passed the shopping centre. It was nearly finished. You couldn't recognize

Grace Park any more. In the middle they were putting up a plinth.

'There's going to be a statue there. Of Ark-wright.'

'Arkwright?'

'He built it.'

'Oh. I hate him.'

'Because he built the shopping centre?'

'Yeah, and because of what his dad did to my grandad. Nobody will ever know about him now,' I said. 'You wouldn't even know there had been a football ground there.' I felt in my inside pocket and brought out a folded piece of newspaper. I opened it and handed it to her. 'That's him,' I said. 'I always carry it with me.'

'I bet he was a good player.'

'Of course he was,' I said.

I stared out of the window at the mass of new buildings.

'We didn't do much to stop it, did we?' she said.

I shook my head. It had all been a waste of time, really.

'We ought to go in there one night and pour white paint over his statue.'

A year ago Frankie would have started planning how we could do it. 'You get the paint,' she'd have said, 'I'll throw some stones at your window at midnight. Wear black clothing, that's very important . . .'

But all she said now was. 'Wouldn't achieve anything. Just make some money for the poor bloke who had to clean the mess up. If you haven't got a good plan you're better off doing nothing at all. If you do something badly you just play into the hands of the enemy.'

I remembered how during the play she'd lied to me, saying she had another idea. But I didn't remind her.

'You never know. Something might come.' She tapped her forehead with her fingers. 'Have to use your brains you see, Benbow.'

She hadn't called me Benbow for a long time.

'I'll keep thinking,' she said.

We got off the bus at Hesketh Bank by the canal. There was a row of small factories. We walked down to one of them. Outside was a sign saying:

O'REILLY AND SON BRASS FOUNDERS
INSCRIPTIONS. STATUETTES

Frankie pushed open a wooden door and we went in. The factory was dark and smelled of oil and polish. There was the noise of a drill. Two men were pouring liquid metal into a mould. Along the walls were broken statues; an angel with only one wing, an eagle from a church with a foot missing. In a corner a man was leaning over a table. He had goggles on and had a sort of electric pencil in his hand. We went over.

'Excuse me,' said Frankie.

The drill was screaming as it cut into the metal. I had to put my hands over my ears.

'EXCUSE ME,' shouted Frankie. The man looked up. He turned off the machine and pushed his goggles on to his forehead.

'How d'you do,' he said. 'What can I do you for?'

He lit a cigarette.

'My mother asked you to do a sign,' said Frankie. 'For her front door. She rang you.'

She gave him the piece of paper with the instructions. He put on a pair of spectacles.

At another table somebody else was hammering and drilling.

'Wilson, wasn't it?' the man shouted. 'She rang me up. I remember now.'

He read the instructions.

I looked round. There were some wooden steps going upwards in the corner. The men had finished pouring the metal into the cast and were taking their gloves and goggles off. There was a smell of metal burning. The man puffed on his cigarette but didn't take it out of his mouth.

'It's going to be a month or more. We've got a load of work on. Look at all this.'

He took a handful of envelopes from a rack on the wall. 'All these to do,' he said. 'Look at this.' He opened the envelope and took out a letter with a drawing. 'This is for the council. Haven't even had time to read it properly yet.' He threw it down on the bench. 'It's for that blasted new shopping plaza in town. A statue and an inscription they want. In six weeks. Six weeks! Who do they think we are? Superman! Expect us to drop everything. That's a ten-week job, that is. When it comes to paying they're not in such a hurry, I'll tell you. What!'

We both nodded sympathetically.

'I'll do my best for her. Tell her that. But I'm not promising nothing.'

He looked around. 'Where's that pencil?'

'Behind your ear,' I said.

'Oh aye.' He took it out and began searching. Turning over pieces of paper. 'Where is the damn thing?' he muttered. 'Can't find nothing in this place. Look, the samples are upstairs. You'll have to come up to the office. Tell her to look at the samples. There's a number against each one. Tell your mum she's to tell me what style. If she gives me the number I'll know what she's on about. She only has to ring me. They're in the office.' He walked towards the stairs and started to climb. We followed. Just as we reached the top, Frankie suddenly stopped.

'Oh,' she said, 'I've left my coat downstairs.' She ran down the stairs again. I followed the man into a windowed office in the corner of the attic. He searched over a large desk and then in some drawers, muttering to himself. At last, he found what he was looking for and we went downstairs. I looked round for Frankie but she was nowhere to be seen.

'Where's she got to?' said the man, scratching his head.

He shouted to his partner. The noise of the drill stopped.

'Did you see a girl in here just now?'

247

'A girl,' said the other man. 'Aye, she was by your table there. Looked like she was looking for something. Then she left.'

'She left? What she do that for? I had this list of samples and prices for her. What's she up to?'

The other man shook his head. Pulled down his goggles and went on drilling.

'I don't know, young people today.' He turned to me. 'Look here, you take this.' He stuck the price list in an envelope, licked and stuck it down. 'Give it to your mother and tell your big sister from me not to run off like that next time.'

'She's not my sister.'

'Not?'

'No.'

'But you know her, don't you? She's your friend, isn't she?'

'Not really,' I said. I wondered what I'd done to make her go off like that. I started to understand what my dad meant when he got exasperated with my mum sometimes. He'd say, 'Women, I don't understand them.'

'I know her, that's all,' I said to the man.

'Well, give her a thick ear from me when you see her, will you? Look, what's her address? I'll have to put this in the post for her. Unless you could take it round for us.'

I didn't want to go round to her house.

'She lives miles away from me,' I said.

I gave him Frankie's address. But I wasn't really thinking what I was doing. I couldn't care less if I never saw Frankie again. I hadn't wanted to come in the first place. I'd just done it to make her feel better. I'd thought she'd wanted to be friendly again. As I walked towards the door and the street, another thought struck me. She hadn't brought a coat with her and she hadn't given the picture of Grandad back. I'd probably never see it again. It was precious, that photograph. I carried it everywhere with me.

As I pulled open the big wooden door I heard the man shouting to his friend. 'Have you seen that envelope from the council? Damn me! I had it a few minutes ago.'

I felt like saying, 'You'd lose your head if it was loose.' But you can't say that to adults, can you? That was something else that wasn't fair. As I got on the bus I made a vow that if Frankie called again I wouldn't speak to her. Ever.

Then, one morning in the Easter holidays, the phone rang. My dad was making dinner for me and Sam. We were watching a quiz programme on the television. Sam kept calling out the wrong answers. When the quiz master gave out the correct ones, he kept saying, 'Said that.' Baby Andrew was asleep upstairs. Dad said, 'It's for you.'

'Who is it?'

'I don't know. Sounds like a lady's voice.'

'I don't know any ladies.'

Sam said, 'You can say that again.'

He was developing a very sharp tongue, was Sam.

I picked up the phone.

Dad said, 'Don't make it very long. Your dinner'll be on the table in a couple of minutes.'

I heard a girl's voice at the other end say, 'Benjie?'

I didn't know who it was. I just said, 'Hello.'

The voice said, 'Don't you know who it is?'

It was Frankie. I shook my head. Then realized it didn't make much sense to shake your head when you're having a telephone conversation.

'No,' I said.

'It's me, Frankie.'

'Frankie?'

Sam made a stupid noise and said 'Frankie' in a daft sort of voice. He kept on saying 'Frankie' and rolled around on the sofa. He was turning into a real pain.

'Shut up you, stupid . . .' I shouted.

'What?' said Frankie.

'Not you,' I said. 'I was talking to Sam.'

There was a silence.

'I bet you're wondering why I'm ringing you up?' Frankie said.

'Not really.'

'I bet you think I'm awful.'

'I don't think about you at all.'

'Oh.'

There was a long pause.

'Is that why you haven't spoken to me at school for two months?'

'Maybe.'

'Is it because I walked out of the factory that time?'

'Maybe.'

'There was a reason. That's why I rang up. I couldn't tell you till now.' There was a pause. 'Don't you want to hear about it?'

'Not particularly,' I said.

'I'm sorry I ran off like that, the last time.'

'I felt really stupid. That man thought you were my sister.'

I could hear her laughing on the other end of the phone. That made me feel worse.

'I'm sorry. I had something to do.'

'Well, I wish you'd told me what it was all about.'

'I will.'

'What?'

'Tell you what it's about.'

I didn't answer but my curiosity was getting the better of me.

'Don't you want to know?'

I could hear the line crackling. She was talking to someone.

'Who are you with?'

'What?'

'I heard you speaking to someone. Who's there?'

I thought it might be Alan Maitland. I thought of them laughing at me on the other end of the

251

phone. I could hear her saying to him, 'And then I just walked out and left him there. I'd have loved to have seen his face.'

'It's just my mum,' she said.

'Oh,' I said. I wasn't sure if I believed her. 'Well, are you going to tell me?'

'Not over the phone,' she said. 'I can't tell you over the phone.'

'Why not?'

'Because I can't. That's all.'

I looked out of the window. My dad was putting some washing out on the line. Baby Andrew was in the pram at his side.

I sighed. 'Well, if you can't tell me now I can't be bothered. I can't be bothered with you, at all. You don't want to play football any more. You told me not to do that speech in the play and it was your idea in the first place. You told Maitland about it when it was nothing to do with him. You stole that picture of my grandad and then you take me to some stupid factory and walk off and leave me there like a spare part. What you think I am, stupid or something?'

I could hear her moving about at the other end of the line. Then she said very calmly.

'I don't think you're stupid, Benjie.'

'You'd never know.'

'People change. They change, that's all.'

'How d'you mean, change?'

'They grow up.'

'You mean I haven't grown up?'

'I didn't mean that, at all. Why don't you give me a chance to explain?'

'I am. I am giving you a chance to explain.'

'Will you come and meet me?'

My dad came in. He started clearing the table.

'I hope we're not paying for this phone call,' he said, cupping his right hand beneath the edge of the table and brushing crumbs into it with the other.

'No.'

'You won't?' said Frankie.

'I was talking to my dad.'

'Oh. Will you come?'

'Where?'

'The new shopping plaza.'

'The new . . . I hate that place. What would I want to go there for? Why can't you tell me now?'

'I just can't. It's important. Honestly. I can't tell you on the phone. Honest. I just can't. You have to believe me. Please come. I'll bring the photograph of your grandad. He'd be pleased if you were there.'

'What's it got to do with him?'

'I can't tell you now. You've got to come. I'll meet you there at three o'clock. Trev'll be there and Carlton and John Stokes. Bring Sam, too. I'll have the photo with me.'

'How do I know you won't make a fool of me like last time?'

'Honest. It'll make up for everything. Will you be there? Please. It's really important. Honestly.'

I put the mouthpiece on my chest and thought about it. I didn't want to see her again and at the same time I did. And I did want the photograph of Grandad back. What could it have to do with him? I hated the shopping precinct. It was full of people and prams and shouting crowds and anyway it reminded me too much of where we used to play and of my grandad.

'Are you there?' she asked.

'I'm here,' I said.

'You'll be there, then?'

'All right.'

'Three o'clock. You're sure you'll be there?'

'Yes, I'll be there. But you'd better . . .' I didn't know what I was going to say. But she seemed to know.

'I won't,' she said. 'Trust me.'

I put the phone down.

The funny thing about it was that I wanted to trust her but I didn't know whether I could or not. Not any more.

18

Outside the main entrance, hanging between two tall pillars, was a huge sign. It said:

WELCOME TO THE NEW ARKWRIGHT SHOPPING PLAZA

The whole town seemed to have decided to do their shopping at the same time. You could hardly move for people. Over to my right, in the distance, I could hear a brass band playing *Colonel Bogey*. I followed the direction of the music. I'd lost all my bearings. When it had been Grace Park you knew exactly where you were. There were the steps on the right, the woods at the bottom and the allotments at the other end. You knew your way round. But now, it was completely different. Now, it just looked like anywhere else. If I hadn't known that they'd built it on Grace Park I would never have guessed. Because we'd played on it as long as I could remember I'd had the feeling Grace Park would always be there. And now it had disappeared as though it had never been. In five years' time if you said anything to young kids about Grace Park they'd probably look at you as if you were daft and say, 'What's that?' It made me feel frightened, angry and sad all at the same time. I kept thinking, we should have done something about it. We'd tried but we hadn't tried hard enough.

They'd planted a row of trees but already one had been broken off and there were newspapers and paper bags blowing all over the place. On one tree two crows were sitting. A couple of big lads went by and threw stones at them and the crows flew off all ragged and black. I had a strange feeling that I'd been here before. That what was happening now had somehow happened before, but I couldn't quite remember when. The two lads ran off shouting and laughing and pushing people out of the way. Then the crows came back.

Suddenly, for no reason, I felt cold and scared. It was like when I was about six and used to have nightmares all the time. I used to be frightened of the dark. I'd lie there wide awake, staring into the blackness screaming for Mum. My dad would come up. He'd ask me what was the matter. But I couldn't tell him because it wasn't really a nightmare. I hadn't dreamed anything. It was just a feeling. It was something to do with believing that the darkness had no end. That it went on for ever and ever. I couldn't tell my dad that. He would have thought I was stupid. Mum would have understood. She was good at understanding things that I couldn't explain. But she wasn't there. She was doing some play or other. Dad would say, she'll come up and see you when she gets back from the theatre. But often she didn't. Or else I'd be asleep.

Walking through the crowds that afternoon I had the same feeling I'd had then. It was really strange. And I found out something. Something for myself. And it's different to find out something for yourself than to have somebody else tell you. Because it's not like your brain understanding it. You seem to understand all over. It comes into your whole body. It was something to do with realizing that if they could change Grace Park then they could change anything. That nothing was for ever. That one day the whole of the country could be one enormous shopping plaza. It was just like that great darkness that used to terrorize me all those years ago. One of the crows croaked and stretched its great black wings. Then I remembered; I remembered what had made me think I'd been here before. It had been Grandad's funeral. The crows had been there, too. Not the same crows, I supposed. In a way, this was a funeral, too. A funeral for Grace Park.

Then Frankie was there. 'Over here,' she called. She looked at me. 'Are you all right?'

'Yes,' I said, 'I'm fine.'

'Well, you don't look it,' she said. 'You were standing like a statue, staring into space.'

I felt embarrassed.

'I was watching those crows,' I said.

Frankie tugged me by the arm. 'Come on,' she said, 'or we'll be late.'

'Late for what?'

But she was gone through the crowds and I was chasing after her.

In the middle of the Plaza there was a semi-circle of steps facing a brick stage. In the middle, surrounded by a low white fence and a flower bed, was a thin sort of tent. The bandsmen were sitting towards the back of the stage dressed in red and blue uniforms. A fat man was conducting them. Every time the baton went above his head he stretched up on his toes; up and down with the music. The spectators were sitting on the stone steps and leaning over the low wall at the back. Above the band was a huge yellow banner and on it was written in big square letters:

The Arkwright Shopping Plaza
Official Opening
3.00 pm Saturday 5th April

I caught up with Frankie. Trev was there and Carlton and John Stokes. It was just like old times.

Carlton said, 'If I'd brought the ball we could have had a kick around.'

'Yeah, all we'd have to do is blow up the whole Plaza,' said Trev.

'You bring the dynamite, I'll bring the matches.'

I stood next to Frankie. There was a strange expression on her face.

'Where's Sam?' she asked.

'He's down the rec.'

'Pity, I wanted us all to be here.'

'For what?'

'You'll see,' she said.

I said, 'Have you ever had a funny feeling that something's happened to you before?'

'Oh yes,' she said. 'I get it all the time. Have you got it now?'

'I did just now.'

'Déjà vû,' she said.

'What?'

'That's what they call it. Déjà vû. It's French.'

I looked at the stage. A man in glasses had arrived. He said 'One, two' into a microphone. It whistled. I wondered what was underneath the tent. Out of the corner of my eye I looked at Frankie.

'I suppose you know everything, don't you?' I said.

'Not everything,' she said. 'Does it annoy you? Would you rather stay ignorant?'

I hadn't forgotten how she'd walked out of that factory. I was still mad at her about that.

'Yeah, well, you don't know everything,' I said.

'I know more than you.'

'Yeah?'

'Yeah.' She mocked my voice but she was smiling.

'Go on,' I said. 'Tell me something I don't know.'

She looked at me. Her cheeks were red and her eyes were wide and shining.

'All right,' she said. 'Tell me what's under there.' She pointed at the tent. The man with glasses was pulling gently at a thin red ribbon that hung down from it.

I shook my head. 'I bet you don't know, either.'

'Bet you I do.'

'You've looked, then.'

She shook her head.

'What is it?'

'You wait and see.'

The crowd to the right parted and two large black cars pulled up at the foot of the stage. The band played louder. The man in glasses rushed down the steps and escorted three men up on to the platform. One was wearing a three-cornered hat and a red gown. Around his shoulders was a heavy chain. Behind him was a tall man I thought I recognized, and bringing up the rear was Mr Braithwaite.

'Eh, that man!' said Trev. 'You remember when we went to the Town Hall that time?'

'Who's the fella in the funny hat?' asked John Stokes.

'The Lord Mayor, dafthead,' said Carlton.

'Old Liversedge,' said Trev, pointing.

There he was, sitting in the front row, looking round to see if he recognized anybody in the crowd. I shuffled behind Carlton. The three men sat down. The Mayor smiled and waved at the crowd. The man in the spectacles leaned over and whispered something into Mr Braithwaite's ear. He nodded and then walked up to the microphone. He tapped on it. It sounded like a hammer. He cleared his throat.

'Ladies and gentlemen,' he said. The people went quiet.

'Ladies and gentlemen. My name is Braithwaite and, as your Town Clerk, it is my duty, nay, my pleasure, to welcome you all here this afternoon. And what a pleasant afternoon it has turned out to be.'

Trev and me booed just loud enough to be heard. Mr Liversedge looked round, his eyes searching crossly.

Mr Braithwaite continued. 'As you may or may not know, this splendid new centre and shopping plaza where you are now standing, with all its fine shops, modern amenities and splendid buildings is the result, in the main, of the determination, persistence and efforts of one man, Sir Gerald Arkwright.'

The Mayor clapped and smiled and looked at the man sitting next to him. He looked at his feet.

'And I would like to call on our Lord Mayor, Councillor Albert Bakewell, to introduce him to us.'

He sat down, and the Lord Mayor came down to the microphone. His face was large and red and he smiled round at everybody.

'Mr Braithwaite is too modest. Too modest by a long chalk. You know if it hadn't been for his efforts we wouldn't be standing here today in this wonderful plaza. He is the man you never see who oils the wheels so that nothing upsets the apple cart.'

Mr Braithwaite looked up at the sky and shook his head.

'Well, you may deny it but it is, nevertheless, a fact. Now, Sir Gerald Arkwright, we have a surprise for you.'

Sir Gerald looked up and Mr Braithwaite smiled at him.

'Yes, indeed, a surprise. Of course, Sir Gerald Arkwright knows that this marvellous amenity will be named after him, and quite properly, too, since it was his firm that was responsible for building it. So, Sir Gerald, if I may be so familiar, would you be kind enough to pull that red ribbon there and underneath the sheet you will find a statue of your good self, sir, with a short, simple and, I think I can say this in all honesty, fitting inscription.'

Sir Gerald looked surprised.

'I bet he knew all along,' whispered Frankie.

Sir Gerald stood up and walked down to the microphone.

'My Lord Mayor, Mr Town Clerk, ladies and gentlemen, thank you for those very kind but, I'm sure, undeservedly flattering, remarks. I would just like to say this. If I take any pride in this enterprise, this fine centre where you are now standing at this moment in time, it is because previously, where we are now standing, there was only an eyesore. A wasteland. And now there is this prestigious amenity.'

'What wasteland?' I said aloud. 'It was Grace Park.' If I'd had a tomato I would have thrown it at him. I felt really mad. I shouted out. 'It was Grace Park!' Mr Liversedge looked round crossly. 'Ssh,' said the lady in front of me.

'It wasn't a wasteland, it was Grace Park.'

Mr Braithwaite frowned in our direction. I didn't care whether he saw me or not, now.

'Ssh, don't spoil it,' said Frankie.

'What you bring me here for to listen to a lot of boring old speeches?'

'Quiet,' said the lady in front.

I saw Mr Liversedge looking at me.

Sir Gerald stuttered. 'Er, yes, er . . . as I was . . . er, saying . . . prestigious amenity. And so I would just like to say this, ladies and gentlemen. If this centre is useful to you, if it advances the reputation of our fine little town, then I will be indeed proud that it was named after me. I therefore take great pleasure in declaring Arkwright Shopping Plaza officially open.'

The band struck up. Mr Braithwaite shook Sir Gerald by the hand and then led him by the arm to the centre of the stage and put the ribbon in his hand. Sir Gerald pulled it and as the white sheet fell away the spectators clapped and cheered and a flock of pigeons flew up into the sky. None of us clapped. Then I looked at the Mayor's face. Something had gone wrong. Sir Gerald's jaw was hanging open and the Lord Mayor's face had gone bright red. The Mayor shouted at Mr Braithwaite and pointed at the bronze statue and the plaque.

I wondered if he was angry because the statue wasn't a good likeness. I couldn't hear what he was saying because he had moved away from the microphone. But he was really mad. Mr Braithwaite was spreading his hands and backing away. For a minute I thought the Mayor was going to hit him. Every now and then they'd go near the microphone and odd words like, 'bungling' and 'incompetent' and 'laughing stock' would ring all round the square. Then the Lord Mayor realized where he was. He turned to the audience and tried to smile. But he couldn't. His mouth went up at the corners. But it wasn't a smile. He even tried to say a few words. The brass band didn't know what they were supposed to do. Some of them had stopped playing. They looked about them with bewildered expressions on their faces.

Mr Braithwaite was backing away from the Mayor. I could hear him saying, 'I'm sorry, I'm sorry,' over and over again. He took hold of the microphone.

'Ladies and, er ladies and er . . .'

But the microphone seemed to have stopped working. The conductor turned to the band and raised his baton and then brought it down. They began to play a very fast march but only half of the band had been watching him. The Mayor shouted something, then strode angrily with Sir Gerald towards one of the big cars, his chin wobbling. Mr Braithwaite chased after them. He tripped on the steps and one or two people started to laugh. He ran towards the car. I heard him calling, 'Sir

Gerald, Councillor Bakewell, let me explain,' but the car pulled away knocking Mr Braithwaite to the ground. He scrambled to his feet and climbed into the second car. It disappeared in a cloud of exhaust gas.

'He fell on the floor,' said Stokesy, screaming with laughter. 'His hair came off. I thought his head had fallen off.' He coughed so much with laughter that I thought he was going to choke.

'What was all that about?' I asked Frankie.

'Come on,' she said and pulled me towards the stage. Mr Liversedge was on his feet and walking through the crowd staring about him. We dodged down amongst the crowd. I saw him disappearing in the direction of the shops. The crowd was beginning to disperse. The band was arguing amongst themselves. Some were putting their instruments into cases. There was a small group of people standing round the statue. I wanted to go home. Frankie had let go my hand and had disappeared into the crowd on the stage. I started to go away.

'I'm going home,' I said. 'I hate crowds.'

She ran after me and caught hold of my arm with both hands.

'Don't you dare,' she said. Her eyes were narrow and her lips were white. 'Don't you dare after what I've done for you.'

'What d'you mean? What have you done?'

She pushed and pulled and butted her way through the crowd until we were at the front.

She turned round, her hands on her hips and her eyes shining.

'There!' she said.

I looked in the direction she was pointing. There was a statue on a block of stone. It was about four feet high. It showed a footballer in baggy shorts kicking a ball.

I looked round at Frankie.

'What is it?' I couldn't understand why the Lord Mayor should want a statue of a footballer.

'Read it,' she said. 'Read what it says.'

Underneath cut into brass was written in large bold letters.

HERE ONCE STOOD GRACE PARK.
IT WAS ON THIS SPOT THAT
ARTHUR BENBOW SCORED THE PENALTY
THAT BEAT EVERTON AND HELPED TAKE
THE TOWN TO THE CUP FINAL AND
TO THE GLORY OF VICTORY AT WEMBLEY

We shall not look upon his like again.

I turned. Trev, Stokesy and Carlton were reading it over my shoulder. Frankie was watching me.

I didn't want to, but tears were coming into my eyes. Somehow I didn't mind.

Stokesy said, slow on the uptake, as usual, 'Arthur Benbow? Isn't he your grandad? Here, Trev, that's his grandad, isn't it?'

I went up to Frankie. She was smiling.

'D'you think your grandad would have been pleased?'

Stokesy was spelling out the words slowly. 'We-shall-not look-upon-his-like-again.'

'It's from Shakespeare,' said Frankie. 'I thought it sounded good.'

'Very good,' I said. 'Very good indeed.'

She pulled her scarf round her neck and buttoned up her overcoat collar. 'I have to be going. I'm leaving, you know. My mother's got a partnership in the south. We'll be moving on after the holidays.'

She put a white envelope in my hand. 'That's for you,' she said and walked off into the crowd.

I opened the envelope. Inside was an Easter card and inside the card a folded newspaper cutting. I opened it up. It was the photograph of Grandad. I looked from the photograph to the statue and back to the photograph. There was no doubt. I looked up and saw Frankie's red head bobbing amongst the crowd. I ran after her. She kept walking.

'When we went to that factory?' I said.

'Yup.'

'You didn't leave your coat.'

'Nope.'

'You went down and . . . How did you get it?'

'Stole it.' She gave a wave of her hand. 'Simply stole it.'

I walked briskly beside her. I had a job keeping up.

'Stole it? The letter from the Town Clerk with the instructions on.'

'Yes, stole it. There it was. One bronze statue of Sir Gerald Arkwright. I didn't think he should have a statue, do you? Not on Grace Park. So I picked it up and ran off with it. Then I changed it. Typed it out on my mother's machine. Made it look proper. Enclosed the photo and sneaked back in and left it on their table. So what do we have?'

'A statue of Grandad.' I shook my head in amazement.

She stopped. We looked at one another. She held up her index finger and laid it on her forehead and tapped it closing one eye.

'Brains, you see,' she said. 'Brains.'

'Brains,' I repeated. I looked at her. 'Are you really going away? Does that mean I won't ever see you again?'

'Yes.' She looked at me steadily with her clear eyes. 'And I shall miss you, Benbow.'

'Are you going for ever?'

She leaned forward and kissed me on the cheek. She whispered in my ear, 'For ever is a long, long time.'

And then she was gone.

I called after her, 'Frankie,' I shouted. 'Frankie, I wanted to tell you something.' I don't know whether she heard me or not. I knew she wouldn't look back. Frankie had always been a great one for not looking back. Soon her red, bouncing head was lost in the crowd.

I stood still and the crowd surged round me.

I put the card in my pocket and looked round for the others but they were nowhere to be seen. I had to get away from all the crowd. I started walking towards the exit and into the streets outside. Then I started running. I ran as far as I could. It felt good to run. The bus was going past. I didn't have any money but I ran alongside it. Then I started to drop back. Upstairs two kids were waving and banging on the windows to get me to go faster but I was out of breath.

Where the road turned in to Windy Harbour Lane, Marion Archard came out of her drive.

I hadn't seen much of her since the play had finished. I hadn't been speaking to anybody much. Normally I would have pretended not to see her. I did that with a lot of people. But this time I stopped.

'You been r-r-running?' she asked.

'Yes,' I said.

'Where you been, then?'

'Been looking at things.'

'What things?'

'A statue.'

'Statue?'

'My grandad. It's in Grace Park. It's got writing under.'

She looked at me. 'I'll have to have a look at that. Will you show me where it is?'

'Sometime.'

'Yeah, sometime.'

I looked at the ground trying to get my breath back.

'G-G-Going any place particular?'

'Nowhere.'

'I'm going to the Grand. They've got these auditions. Want to come along? You were good in the play.'

'I don't know.' I looked over towards the rec. I could hear the thump of a football being kicked. 'I might.'

'Oh well. Just as you like,' she said.

I looked up at her. I'd never looked at her properly before. I'd always thought of her as someone who stuttered. That was all. In the same way that I thought of Sandra Ollerenshaw as someone who was fat. She was looking for her bus money. She had freckles and her eyes looked wide open and worried.

'I've just noticed,' I said.

'What?'

'You've stopped stuttering.'

'Sometimes I don't. It's when I'm nervous.'

I walked alongside her.

At the bus stop we sat down. She didn't seem to mind not talking. She looked at me and smiled and then looked away again. She was all right. I wondered if she might lend me the bus fare. The bus came round the corner.

'Are you coming, then? It's the last day. I'll lend you the bus fare. Have to pay me back, though.'

I thought about it. 'No,' I said, 'I've got money. I think I'll play football.'

She got on the bus.

270

'See you then,' she said, smiling.

'See you.'

She went upstairs. I saw her sitting on her own in the back seat. Just before it went round the corner I saw her looking round. Then it was gone.

As I walked down to the rec I kept getting this picture of her. The way she'd looked at me and smiled and looked away again.

Sam and some kids his own age were kicking a ball about. Sam was running down the wing nearest to me. His hair was wet and over his eyes. There was mud all over his shoes.

'You'll catch it if Dad sees those shoes,' I shouted. He kept on running.

'You playing?' he asked.

'I don't know.' They all looked young.

The ball bounced over to me. I belted it as hard as I could. It skidded off the side of my shoes and over into the car park by Lancaster's Dairy.

'Ya hopeless,' shouted one of the kids.

'We're Brazil,' said Sam. 'It's seven all. It's the tenth replay.'

One of the kids shouted, 'Come on, Sam.'

He looked over. 'Coming?' he shouted.

I said, 'Can you lend us twenty-five pence?'

He searched in his pocket and laid the coins in my hand.

'I'll pay you back,' I said.

'I know you will.'

I walked across the field to the bus stop. After

five minutes a bus came along. I got on and sat by the door. Then I went upstairs and sat in the back seat.

It was worth a try, I thought.

The ticket collector came round.

'Single to the Grand,' I said.